I'm Deborah Sampson

A Soldier in the War of the Revolution

Books by Patricia Clapp

Constance:
A Story of Early Plymouth

Dr. Elizabeth:
The Story of the First Woman Doctor

I'm Deborah Sampson:
A Soldier in the War of the Revolution

Jane-Emily

King of the Dollhouse

I'm Deborah Sampson

A Soldier in the War of the Revolution

Patricia Clapp

Lothrop, Lee & Shepard Co.
A Division of William Morrow & Co., Inc. ☆
New York

For my daughter Pat,
with love,
in exchange for Deborah.

 Inquiries should be addressed to Lothrop, Lee & Shepard Company, 105 Madison Ave., New York, N. Y. 10016. Printed in the United States of America.
1 2 3 4 5 6 7 8 9 10
Library of Congress Cataloging in Publication Data
Clapp, Patricia.
I'm Deborah Sampson.
SUMMARY: Relates the experiences of the woman who disguised herself as a man in order to enlist and fight in the American Revolution.
1. Gannett, Deborah Sampson, 1760-1827—Juvenile fiction. [1. Gannett, Deborah Sampson, 1760-1827—Fiction. 2. United States—History—Revolution, 1775-1783—Fiction] I. Title.
PZ7.C5294Ian [Fic] 76-51770
ISBN 0-688-41799-X ISBN 0-688-51799-4 lib. bdg.

Author's Note

In the various accounts of Deborah Sampson's life there are differences in certain details, such as names and dates. Since this is a story and not a biography, I have selected arbitrarily from among the sources available to me.

I should like to thank Miss Pauline Moody and Mrs. Robert J. Cartwright, both of Sharon, Massachusetts, for their kind help and cooperation in furnishing background material and educated opinions which were invaluable.

P.C.

Table of Contents

First Thoughts

Occasionally, even now, people are brought to meet me who have heard of my early history. There they stand, facing a tall, average-looking woman whose years are adding up, and on their faces I read polite, but open disbelief. "This one?" I can almost hear them thinking. "*This* one? Disguised as a man? Fighting as a soldier—killing Redcoats? Unsuspected and undiscovered? Impossible!"

I cannot blame them. Even to me it often seems an unlikely tale which must have happened to someone else. It was all so long ago, and it is becoming harder to remember now. That is why I have decided to record it all—how it was to be shifted from home to lonely home, to be bound out to a family with ten sons. Jouncing over uncharted country in a Conestoga wagon, or invited to tea by a lovely young girl. The shameful disgrace in a public tavern, the terror of being buried alive. And love . . . and loss . . . and pain . . .

Whatever I am now, these things have made me. Lest I lose it all—the good, or the evil—the worth, or the waste—now, before it is too late, let me set it down.

Because for all of us time runs out, sooner or later.

Although in the year 1765, when I was just a chit—not six years old—I would never have believed it. . . .

1 ☆ "I'm Deborah Sampson"

It is almost as if I can look back and see her, that child named Deborah, who made herself as small as possible and lay curled behind the heavy door, listening to the voices of her mother and her Cousin Ruth Fuller. Mrs. Sampson's voice was ragged with tears, as it so often was of late. Cousin Fuller's voice was as dry and thin as the little old lady herself.

"I can't keep them all, Cousin. I can't feed them!"

"That Jonathan!" Cousin Fuller sounded indignant. "What call did he have to go running off to sea? He should be here, supporting his family!"

"I know. But he was so angered—Jon always felt he should have had a larger share in his father's will. He believed far too much went to his brother-in-law."

"That was no reason to sell his own share of land to his sisters and turn tail and run! He could have put that land to good use!"

"Jon doesn't like farming. He never has. He always wanted to go to sea."

"If he'd *stay* at sea you'd be better off. Every time he comes home for a few days he leaves you with another baby on the way and no money to care for it. Men!

Huh!" Deborah could hear Cousin Fuller's dry sniff of scorn.

"Men cannot help it, Cousin. You'd feel differently if you had ever wed one."

"No doubt I would. And if one had ever asked me when I was young and foolish, I might be in your state now. Thank the good Lord no one did! You will have to scatter the children, Deb."

Mrs. Deborah Sampson sighed. Behind the door the five-year-old Deborah listened, her breath held tight.

"I've tried mightily to keep them together, Cousin —but it's the food! I can't raise much without help— and there are things I *have* to buy! Six cents a pound for butter yesterday, and twelve for meat! The children are growing. They need to be properly fed."

There was a tiny silence before Cousin Fuller's dry little voice spoke firmly. "I shall take Deborah. She seems a good child, and bright. I'll do my best with her, Deb."

"Oh, Cousin!" Deborah knew her mother's tears were flowing again. "She *is* good, and she *is* bright. She can read a bit already. She is willful sometimes, but she is a loving child."

"She must earn her keep."

"Oh, she will! I am sure she will! But how can I let her go?"

"Don't be foolish, Deb. You can see her as often as you like. It is not as though we lived miles apart."

"You are right, of course. It's just that . . . I love them all, but Deborah . . . she has so much spirit! She does my heart good!"

"I will try to direct that spirit into God's ways, Cousin Deb. It does not do for a woman to have too much of it."

Young Deborah set her bright hazel-colored eye against the crack in the door and saw her mother wiping tears away with the corner of her apron. She wished that she could run and hide somewhere—someplace where Cousin Fuller could not find her and take her away. To leave home, to leave her mother and Sylvia and Ephraim and little Nehemiah . . . not to see her strong, ruddy father when he came home on those infrequent visits, smelling of salt and tar, and excitingly boisterous . . . to be set in "God's ways" by dried-up Cousin Fuller. . .

But she was trapped behind the door and there was no escape.

Deborah did not cry when she left her mother. She set her lips tight and clutched the little packet of clothes and belongings close to her as she raised her face for her mother's kiss.

"I will see you often, Deb—I promise. And you will be a good girl, won't you? And do all that kind Cousin Fuller asks of you?"

"Yes, Mam."

"And you will remember to say your prayers and keep your hair neat?"

"Yes, Mam."

"And to be grateful that you have such a generous relative—one who will take you in and provide for you."

"Yes, Mam."

Tears flooded her mother's eyes again, and Miss Fuller spoke warningly. "Now, Deb. It is the only way, you know."

"I know."

"Then come along, Deborah. We will go now." Miss Fuller reached for the small hand.

"Wait, just one moment." Mrs. Sampson went to the shelf above the hearth and reached behind a brass candlestick, drawing out a bit of paper. Kneeling in front of her daughter, she held it out. "Take this, Deborah, and keep it always. I wrote it for you. The rhyme is not much, but perhaps it will help you sometimes."

"What is it?"

"I'll read it to you. It says,

'I'm Deborah Sampson, I'm strong and I'm free.
My forefathers handed their strength down to me.
John Alden, Miles Standish, helped settle this land,
And Governor Bradford ruled well that small band.
Abraham Sampson, he followed ere long,
And all of these names make me loyal and strong.' "

Mrs. Sampson folded the paper and tucked it into Deborah's pocket. Then she cupped her daughter's grave face in her two hands. "Those men were your great-great-grandfathers, daughter. My name was Deborah Bradford before I wed your father, you know that. They were all great men, child—they started a new world here and saw it prosper and grow. They knew hardships far more severe than I hope you will ever know, and they triumphed over them. If things go wrong for you, think of those men, Deborah. Maybe they will give you such strength as they had." The eyes of mother and small daughter met, then Mrs. Sampson kissed the child once more before she rose to her feet. "Now go. Go quickly! And God keep you!"

Deborah did not look back as she walked out of the door with Cousin Fuller. Her free hand was clasped tightly about the paper in her pocket, and already her mind was going over and over the words.

"I'm Deborah Sampson. . . ."

2 ☆ Cousin Fuller

Life with Cousin Fuller was lonely, but not unpleasant. It was filled with chores, of course, but that was natural for any child in the mid-1760s. In the little village of Plympton, near Plymouth, Massachusetts, most folk had farms, either large or small. All Cousin Fuller could manage was a little vegetable plot, which I—that small Deborah—tended as best I could, and a few chickens, for which I scattered the dry, powdery corn and from which I gathered the eggs.

That was how I learned my numbers, for Cousin Fuller was determined to give her charge some education, though she might not be able to give her open affection.

"Go to the hen house, Deborah, and fetch me four brown eggs and two white ones. How many will that be?"

And I would hide my hands behind my back, count four fingers on one and two on the other, and then count them all again.

"Six," I would say proudly, and then run off to get the eggs and prove it.

I learned reading from Cousin Fuller's family Bible.

It was far too heavy for me to lift or hold, so I stood beside the table on which it rested, wending my uncertain way through the strange words in the large print. Sometimes Cousin Fuller would write my name in her neat, precise script and then give me the quill so I could copy it. *Deborah Sampson*. The *b* and the *h* were the hardest and often turned out looking the same.

My mother came to see me fairly often, carrying the youngest baby in her arms with the next oldest clinging to her skirts, and at each visit I would greet her with the certainty that this time she would tell me I was to return home with her. Instead she would smooth my pale fly-away hair, look deeply into my eyes, allow me to hold and play with my newest sibling, and ask me how I did. And as the visits went on, becoming less frequent over the months, I learned never to let my hope be apparent, but simply to answer her questions politely, kiss her gently without throwing my eager arms around her neck, and watch dry-eyed as she left me and walked away homeward. It must have been equally hard for her, but that I did not realize then.

After a year or so we had almost lost the ability to talk together. There was nothing to say except for routine questions about my health, what I was learning, and whether I was making myself useful to Cousin Fuller. I told myself that it was better to be the only child in a house than one of several. If I had no other children to laugh and play and share the joys and secrets of youth with, at least I had a presentable frock to wear, plenty to eat, and a bed of my own in which to sleep—and weep with loneliness.

I know I was not a pretty child. I suppose *plain* is the best word to describe the Deborah I was then. Tall for my age, but not gawky, with large hazel eyes under level brows, straight light hair, and a firm mouth. I was not the sort of little girl one wants to fondle and cosset, and even had I been, Cousin Fuller was not the cosseting kind. I was scolded occasionally, but never physically punished, and my life was comfortable if empty of love and young companionship. I fared better than many children. But there were times when I was filled with far more energy than could be expended in my simple daily chores. Then I longed fiercely for someone to play with, to laugh and run and shout with. Cousin Fuller always knew when I was restless.

"Put your thoughts on God, Deborah," she would say. "Think earnestly on His goodness and learn to walk quietly in His grace."

And I would say "Yes, Cousin Fuller," and wonder why God might think it wrong to run.

Neighbors were not close geographically in those days, since almost every house was surrounded by pastureland, farmland, or both. But they were close socially, and Cousin Fuller did not lack for friendships. Two or three times a week some woman would stop for a cozy chat, or with a pail of fresh milk to exchange for having a letter written (for Cousin Fuller's penmanship was exquisite and many of the women could not write at all), or for some other neighborly reason. One of the most frequent visitors was a Widow Thatcher. Although she lived a few miles away in Middleborough, portly, red-faced Mistress Thatcher on her well-fed, aging bay mare was a familiar sight. In the saddle she closely resembled an over-filled meal bag, and she was never known to travel at more than a leisurely amble. A Christian, God-fearing woman, the widow of Reverend Peter Thatcher who had served for many years in the church most of the families attended, and the mother of another minister, she was well past seventy when I first knew her, but still felt responsibility for the lives of all of her late husband's parishioners.

When I was close to eight years old, Cousin Fuller took ill. The winter was a bitter one, and no matter how close frail Cousin Fuller sat to the fire, she seemed never to get warmed through. Frightened, I tried to care for her. I tucked shawls about her, filled basins with hot water so she could soak her icy feet, and fed her with the decoctions she brewed and kept in thick brown bottles on the top shelf of the kitchen cupboard, which I could only reach by climbing on a tall stool. Her thin chest was racked by every breath and her constant coughing was agony for both of us, but no amount of pleading from me would persuade her to take to her bed.

"If I do that, child, I shall never get out of it again. No, just let me sit here by the fire. I like to watch the flames."

When Mistress Thatcher called, I was relieved to have her to make the decisions and lift responsibility from me. It took her only a few minutes to spread Cousin Fuller's bed with fresh linen, pile it with quilts from the chest, wrap stones—heated in the fire—in clean rags and push them to the foot of the bed to warm it, and then firmly tuck Cousin Fuller in. It was difficult to argue against Mistress Thatcher at any time, and poor Cousin Fuller had not even the strength to try. What little she had was devoted to drawing her next breath.

For a while I sat on the edge of the high bed, holding Cousin Fuller's small, hot, dry hand in mine, while the Widow Thatcher bustled about the kitchen, slamming pots and clattering spoons. My fragile, leaf-dry cousin turned her head and looked at me.

"You are such a good girl, Deborah. What is to become of you now, I wonder?"

"I shall be all right," I said firmly, not having the least idea in the world whether I would or not. "You are not to fret. You must just get well again. *Please* get well!"

And then Mistress Thatcher was back in the chamber carrying a mug of some steaming posset.

"You may leave the room now, child," she said. "Tidy up the kitchen a mite, if you will. I seem to have spilled a little milk on the floor."

So I slid off the bed and went into the kitchen, and with rags and sand scrubbed large puddles of milk from the stone floor. Another neighbor came to the door carrying an earthenware bowl of custard, and asked for Cousin Fuller.

"She has taken to her bed," I said. "Mistress Thatcher is with her."

"I'll just slip in for a moment and see how she is. Poor soul, neither chick nor child to bid her farewell!"

I wanted to say that I might not be a chick, but I was most certainly a child, and I could say farewell quite nicely, but why should I, when the visitor disappeared into the chamber, closing the door behind her. After a few moments Mistress Thatcher came out, her face solemn, her dark beady eyes, almost lost in her fleshy cheeks, searching my face.

"Sit down, child. I want to talk to you."

"But I should be with Cousin Fuller, ma'am."

"There is nothing you can do for her, Deborah. The neighbors will tend her now. It won't be for long."

I looked up at her. "What do you mean?"

"She has the scent of death about her. The dear Lord knows I should recognize it by now! Sit down, Deborah."

There was a little cricket stool by the hearth and I sat there, folding my hands in my lap and putting my feet close together. The fire was hot on my left shoulder, but my right shoulder shivered. All my insides seemed to shiver, too.

"Is she really going to die?" I asked, and my voice trembled. I knew little of death, and the mystery of it frightened me.

"Yes, Deborah. I believe her time has come, and the good Lord in his wisdom will take her from all earthly stress and sit her on His right hand. It is not a cause for mourning, child, but a moment of triumph for her."

I tried to envision frail Cousin Fuller sitting on God's right hand, which seemed uncomfortable for both of them, but the Widow Thatcher was speaking again.

"I am taking you home with me, Deborah. I have spoken to your cousin and she has agreed."

"But . . . but why should I not live with my mother and father again?"

"Your mother has found homes for your brothers and sisters, except for the babies—and she has barely enough to care for them. As for your father——" She paused, and then went on determinedly. "Your father is dead."

I could feel my heart kick hard against my ribs, and I looked up at the Widow Thatcher quickly. "Dead?" I repeated. "But how?"

"He was drowned at sea."

My small world shook. Heaven knows I had not seen much of my father for years, but I remembered. I could hear his laugh, smell the exciting scent that was peculiarly his, feel how strong his hands were when he lifted me. I wanted very much to cry, but not in front of the Widow Thatcher, so I pinched my lips together, squinched my eyes, and stared at my tightly folded hands. My fingernails needed cleaning. There was a little silence until I could trust my voice, and then I said softly, "Why did my mother not tell me?"

"She has been distraught, Deborah. And with the babies to care for—there is another on the way now, your father was home six months ago—how she will make do is a question for God to answer, although everyone helps her as he can. I saw her not two days since, and she was worried about Miss Fuller's health. We discussed this possibility, and she saw it as I did, that you should go with me. It is, after all, only my

Christian duty. Your mother was most grateful."

She stopped talking and waited for me to say something, but I could not speak. I shrank from the thought of living with Mistress Thatcher, with her loud voice, her stout body, and her little half-hidden eyes. At least my Cousin Fuller had been a relative, she had been family of a sort—I could talk of my mother to her, and of my sisters and brothers. If I had lain curled tight in my bed some nights, aching with loneliness and crying softly, missing the familiar warmth of my sister Sylvia's small body tucked close to mine; if I had had to stifle my yearning for playmates—for a chance to unleash the sometimes overpowering need for strenuous physical activity—nevertheless I had been secure and safe. I had come to know the quiet, staid routine of the little house and the dull, uneventful days. But now? To change that known life for an unknown one, to move farther away from my mother, to live under the stern eye of this awesome woman? Every inch of me wanted desperately to run from the house, to race straight to the comfort of my mother's arms. But there was no longer comfort even there. For a second time she had given me away. And she had been "most grateful."

"Have you nothing to say, Deborah?" Mistress Thatcher asked.

I swallowed hard, learning with certainty for the first time that when there is no choice at all you do what you have to do.

"You are most kind, Mistress Thatcher," I murmured. And then, because I knew I should, I added in a whisper, "Thank you."

3 ☆ Mistress Thatcher and the Reverend

Mistress Thatcher's "Christian duty" was very important to her. Having taken me into her home (though never into her heart) she was determined to set me on a path that her God would approve. My physical being was scoured almost raw with strong soap and cold water, my pale hair was strained back so tightly my eyes slanted. My few frocks, which I outgrew rapidly, were clean, serviceable, and unbecoming. There was to be no excuse for the sin of vanity in Mistress Thatcher's house!

I was fed plainly, lest food become a pleasure of the flesh, and nourishingly, lest that flesh weaken and become unable to work. The same plain, nourishing meal served day after day can discourage the appetite of even the healthiest child.

Mistress Thatcher's only reading matter was the Bible—even heavier than Cousin Fuller's—and therefore that was all I was allowed to read also. I was required to memorize long passages from it, and my penmanship lessons were restricted to copying from it. If I can form the letters of "In the beginning God created the heaven and the earth" more precisely than I can those of my own name, it is not surprising. After all, my name has changed several times—the Bible has not.

Her closest friend was Reverend Sylvanus Conant, who had been chosen to fill the pulpit of the First Congregational Church of Middleborough after the death of Reverend Thatcher. She admired and respected the man, and in her eyes he could do no wrong.

Reverend Conant called upon us often, and his visits became the closest thing I knew to real happiness. He was a deep-voiced, mild-mannered, blue-eyed man, who—for reasons of his own—took an interest in me. The first time he listened to one of my recitations from the Bible—delivered at Mistress Thatcher's request to prove, I suppose, my spiritual progress under her care —he praised me! Praised *me!* I was so carried away that I rattled off a dozen more passages before I could be firmly silenced by Mistress Thatcher.

"That will do, Deborah!"

Sylvanus Conant smiled at me warmly. "What an astonishing memory you have, child!" he said. "After all my years in the pulpit I could not recite as well as you have just done."

"Do not flatter the child, Sylvanus," Mistress Thatcher said. "Her memory is a God-given gift, and nothing she should have credit for."

Reverend Conant gave me a quick glance filled with gentle mischief before turning to his hostess. "Certainly her *teacher* should have credit," he said smoothly. "Your tutelage and patience are praiseworthy, my dear friend. To have taught your ward so much, and so well——"

With amazement I watched the woman's ruddy face become even redder with embarrassed pleasure. Her lips curved in a little smirk. "Ah, well. The child is not stupid," she said. "It is only Christian to help her brain expand and let in the teachings of God."

That dear man! With so few words he had given me my first pride in myself, and robbed Mistress Thatcher of criticism. There was nothing I would not have done for him, and I set myself the task of learning the Catechism of the Assembly of the Divines. When next he called I delivered it faultlessly, and stood back, glowing. He gazed at me gravely, but there was again that small shine of laughter in his eyes.

"Incredible!" was his pronouncement. "At this rate you will have memorized every word of the sacred writings before you're grown." He turned to Mistress Thatcher. "I am sure you will agree that such devotion to the study of Holy Writ should be rewarded," he said.

The poor woman was taken aback. "Rewarded? A reward for being dutiful?"

"That recitation was more than duty. A most creditable ambition, rather. To discipline one's young mind to such lengths—surely you, too, feel it should be encouraged in some small way. And if you would permit me——"

Though she might disagree privately, there was naught Mistress Thatcher could do but acquiesce with grace. As the Reverend rose to take his leave, she said to me, "Deborah, you may accompany Reverend Conant to the door, and thank him for his interest in you." It was the first time she had granted me a privilege, instead of giving me an order.

Once at the door, the friendly man seemed in no haste to depart. Moving outside onto the broad stone doorstep, he casually eased himself down to sit upon it.

"Such a pleasant day," he said. "Sit down, Deborah, and talk with me. Do you study nothing but churchly writings, child?"

"I like to learn things, and the Bible is the only book I have ever read." I hesitated, and then added bravely, "I do know one other verse—my mother wrote it for me when I was small. When I first had to . . . to leave home. Would you like to hear it?"

"Very much."

"I'm Deborah Sampson, I'm strong and I'm free," I began, and went on through the few lines. When I finished Sylvanus Conant sat looking at me quietly.

"What a fortunate girl you are," he said presently, "having all those strong, worthy men behind you. They form a bulwark on which you can lean."

"But they are all dead! There is nothing they can do for me!"

"They have already done it."

I looked at him, puzzled. "I don't understand, sir. What have they done?"

Reverend Conant took my hand, opening out the fingers and spreading it flat on his knee. "Look at your hand," he told me. "See the long fingers? The strong, wide palm? From one of those men or their wives you got a hand shaped just this way. Your eyes. Hazel, they're called, with a lot of blue in them. They are like your mother's eyes, and hers are probably like the eyes of one of her parents. And just as you have inherited the shape of your hands, or the color of your eyes from your ancestors, so you inherit their strengths and weaknesses."

I pondered that for a moment. "And those men—William Bradford and John Alden and Miles Standish and Abraham Sampson—they were strong men, weren't they, sir?"

"Incredibly strong. They built a new country with nothing more than their hands, their hearts, and their brains. *And* their faith."

"And I have that strength in *me?* From them?"

"Don't *you* think you have?" he asked.

And quite suddenly I did. Behind me there were strong men, and beside me a friend who believed in me. I might be lonely, but I was not entirely alone. Exhilarated, smiling, I stood up from the step, stood as tall as I could.

"Yes!" I said. "Yes, I *can* be strong! I *can!*" And then, because he was such a nice man and I had so longed to show physical affection, I threw both arms around his neck and hugged him as hard as I could. "Oh, thank you, Reverend Conant! Thank you *very* much!"

He gave a little gasp. I must have been hugging him tighter than I thought. "If it is strength you're wanting, Deborah, never fear! You have all kinds!"

My reward for learning the Catechism was a small package containing two books. My own books! The first possessions I had ever had, save for my clothing, a comb, and the verse from my mother. Mistress Thatcher surveyed them doubtfully.

"*Plays* by William Shakespeare? Are you sure this is a proper book for a child, Sylvanus?"

"Oh yes, indeed! Extremely moral and uplifting. Deborah will learn a great deal from Mr. Shakespeare's writings."

"Well, if you are sure . . . but what about this other volume? *Mourt's Relation.* Who is Mourt?"

"No one knows, my friend. But I thought the book might interest Deborah since it is the journal of the Pilgrims at Plymouth. Her ancestors are mentioned frequently. It may make them seem more alive to her." He leaned toward Mistress Thatcher and spoke softly. "An excellent source of history—which, as we *both* know, every child should study."

"Oh, a sort of schoolbook! Then I am sure it will be all right. After all, if *you* chose them, Sylvanus——"

"Exactly," he said, smiling at his hostess. I could have sworn he winked at me!

Somehow things seemed easier after that. The many demands Mistress Thatcher made I could meet with a new trace of inner strength. I learned to answer when spoken to, to keep my voice low, my back straight, and my clothing neat. I learned to repress my frequent overwhelming desire for physical action, and move quietly instead, sewing, mending, or cooking. I learned to avoid Mistress Thatcher's displeasure by making myself promptly available for her endless requests.

"Deborah, fetch the brown embrocation and rub my knee. It does pain me so!"

"Deborah, I'd fancy an egg mixed with milk and a little sugar. It might ease my stomach. And grate the nutmeg over the top."

"Deborah, I cannot sleep. Bring the Bible and read to me."

I stole a candle and, when the Bible had done its work and Mistress Thatcher snored comfortably in her bed, I huddled in mine, shivering when Lady Macbeth tried in vain to cleanse her hands of blood, weeping with the young Romeo and Juliet, and—above all—reading avidly of my great-great-grandfather, William Bradford, and of his determined, successful struggle to build a free world. If he could go through such hardships, then so could I! I was *strong!* The line Mother had written about my being "free" I was not so sure of.

4 ☆ Deborah Bound

When I was ten Mistress Thatcher's health failed rapidly. It seemed as if I spent every waking moment—and many interrupted sleeping ones—in fetching and carrying. Like Cousin Fuller, she refused to take to her bed, but huddled by the kitchen hearth, wrapped in shawls and thinking of things for me to do. The only respite was when Reverend Conant came to call. Then she would talk to him (while I baked the bread), tell him all her ailments (while I brewed the tea), and discuss his next sermon (while I scoured the pots).

One mild spring afternoon he asked me to sit with them for a few minutes. Nothing could have pleased me more, and I perched on the edge of a rush-seated chair, happy to be near this man I called my friend. He and Mistress Thatcher eyed each other, and then the Reverend spoke.

"Deborah," he said, "Mistress Thatcher has decided to make a change. She is going to live with her son and his family. She feels that her advancing years have diminished her health and she would prefer to spend whatever time God allows her in a home where she can be cared for and tended."

That hurt deeply—to have Reverend Conant, the one person I had felt believed in me, feel that I had not taken proper care of that demanding old woman! I *had!* I had done all that anyone could have done. I was sure of it! My voice quavered when I said, "But *I* have cared for her! I have tended her!"

The Reverend leaned forward and took my hand. "Indeed you have, and no one else could have managed any better. But there still comes the desire to be with one's own flesh and blood, to spend one's last years with one's family. I am sure you can understand that, Deborah."

Oh, dear heaven, how well I understood! I was ten years old, a knobby-kneed, sometimes clumsy child. My second teeth seemed too large for my mouth, all my clothes were too small, my hands and feet too large. I was unattractive and knew it. I was unloved, and knew that, too. But my mother was still my mother. She, at least, might love me for myself, not for my appearance. If I could go home to her—no matter how poor we might be—it would be *home!* Family. A place to belong. For one beautiful instant I truly believed it could happen.

"And I will go back to my mother?" I asked, and my voice was filled with hope.

There was a sharp silence in which that hope crumbled to nothingness. The Reverend released my hand, rose, and walked a few steps away. Even Mistress Thatcher's little eyes avoided mine.

"Your mother cannot take you," she began. "As it is, she lives on the charity of neighbors."

Turning, facing me from across the room, the Reverend spoke over her. "We know you would like to be back with your mother, Deborah, but that would be placing a greater burden on her than she could carry, and you would not want that. I have talked to your mother, and she agrees that you need a home where you will be cared for, educated, and taught the domestic skills. I have deliberated at length on this, and I have chosen a family with whom I am sure you will be content." He paused, cleared his throat, and then added, "Your mother has bound you to them—for eight years."

For a moment I was too stunned to speak. Then, *"Bound?"* I whispered.

Sylvanus Conant's voice was gentle. "Yes, Deborah."

"Bound? For eight years? Until I am . . . *eighteen?*"

"Yes, Deborah." He started to move toward me. "Deborah. Please, child. Try to understand."

But I turned away, betrayed. "No! No! Leave me alone—please, leave me alone!"

I could not face them. I could not face anyone. For the third time my mother had *disposed* of me. For eight years, until I was grown, and could no longer be a problem to her. If she had loved me—wanted me—we could have managed somehow! And not only my mother, but the one person I had felt was my friend, Reverend Conant. He, too, was ridding himself of me. He had found some other place for me. He had done his duty—his *Christian* duty—and now there would be some other old woman for me to wait on, run errands for, be ordered about by. My eyes were hot with tears

I could not hold back—would not even try to hold back!—and my throat was so tight I could not speak. Besides, what was there to say? I felt Sylvanus Conant's warm hand on my shoulder and tried, in my utter loneliness and misery, to shrug it off, but it remained. His fingers pressed against my boniness, and I knew he could feel my sobs and I did not care.

"Deborah, have faith in me. You know I am fond of you, child—you *do* know that, don't you?"

I would not answer. I would not even nod. Of what use was his fondness for me? There was no one who cared for Deborah Sampson except Deborah Sampson, and of what good could she be? I stood mute, my face turned stubbornly away.

"Deborah, I want only what is best for you. I am your friend. You *must* believe it! It was I who chose Deacon Thomas's family—it was I who made all the arrangements—and I do sincerely believe they are for the best. Now gather your things together, my girl. I am riding you there this afternoon."

And with a gentle push he started me toward the door to my chamber.

I rode pillion behind the Reverend on the way to the Thomas farm. The tears had run dry, but never had I felt such a weight of abject woe. I was nothing and no one—simply a creature to be bandied round by grown-ups, to be housed wherever someone could be found to take me in. Although I felt him to be a traitor, I could not help but lean my cheek against the Reverend's firm back, seeking some shred of comfort. He was the last tie I had with anything familiar. Even the hoofbeats of his placid mare seemed to repeat "Bound out . . . bound out . . . bound out," as we jogged along. By the time we stopped in front of a neat farmhouse I felt empty, drained, uncaring of what might be in store for me. Where were those strong forefathers now when I needed them? Whatever strength I might once have thought I had was gone. Reverend Conant dismounted and I slid down into his arms.

"It will be all right, Deborah, I promise," he said softly, and then knocked on the farmhouse door. When it opened he pushed me gently ahead of him.

The woman who stood there had a rosy, smiling face and a small, plump figure. The apron over her blue dress circled a firm waist, and a few dark curls escaped from her white ruffled cap.

"Deborah!" she said. "You have come! How glad I am to see you! Come in, child. We are just about to sup."

She stood back that I might step in the door. The late afternoon sun that slanted in behind me lit the bright kitchen, reflecting on the copper pots and kettles. A long table stretched almost the length of the room, and at its head sat a jolly-looking man who smiled at me. On both sides of the table were more boys of all ages than I had ever before seen. As I entered they shuffled to their feet, banging against the table and knocking the benches back in their young awkwardness.

"These are our sons, Deborah," Mrs. Thomas said. "They are noisy, and careless, and not as tidy as they should be. They eat all the time and are constantly growing out of their clothes. But they are good-hearted boys, and they have been looking forward as much as their father and I to having a young sister in the house. I hope you will like them, Deborah, for they already like you."

I remember as if it were yesterday. There were so many of them! They stood quiet, looking at me, and my eyes went from face to face. It had been so long since I had seen young people. How would they take to me? Would they accept me? Hate me? Hurt me? Would this new life be intolerable—or wonderful? I stood as straight as I could, my back stiff, my hands clasped tightly lest they shake from nerves. From halfway along the table a boy with hair like gold and eyes as blue as cornflowers made a small gesture toward me.

"I'm Robbie," he said. "There is room here for you, Deborah—next to me. Are you hungry?"

Somehow tears sprang to my eyes again, but this time—relief? Happiness? I nodded, and moved toward him. From behind me Reverend Conant spoke.

"I shall be calling soon to be sure all is well with you, Deborah. But I think it will be."

I turned to him quickly, blinked my eyes hard, and gave a mighty sniff to dispose of the tears, and then I pressed my forehead tight against his chest.

"I think so, too, sir," I whispered. "Oh, thank you!"

And then I went round the table and settled down to supper in the space the boys had made for me.

5 ☆ The Thomases

At first it seemed I would never know one brother from the next, but in a very few days it was as though I had known them always. At eighteen Nathaniel was the oldest and the most serious, with the dark eyes and hair and snubbed nose that all the boys had except Robbie and the twins. After Nat came Jonathan, the biggest tease, and with the merriest eyes. Then Phineas, then Benjamin, and then Ephraim, all solidly built boys bearing a great physical similarity to each other.

After Ephraim came Robert. Robbie, two years older than I, who had first held out his hand to me. Even at twelve he showed signs of becoming taller than the others, and his voice was softer, not yet deepened into a man's voice, but clear and gentle.

Samuel, who was eleven and who had a slight stammer in moments of excitement, followed Robert, and then the nine-year-old twins, James and David, with hair not quite as gold as Robbie's, but with eyes just as blue. At eight Jeremiah was the youngest, always bearing some proud scar from trying to emulate his older brothers in everything they did.

From the very first I was especially drawn to Robbie,

but every one of them delighted and excited me. To be part of a large and youthful household was new and precious, and each day held challenges and adventures. I wanted so much to have them like me—not to look down on me because I was a girl.

"Deb, put that axe down! You'll chop your hand off!" Nathaniel roared.

"If you can chop wood, so can I!"

"I vow you are the most stubborn female ever I knew! Well, if you must try, at least learn how! Here, hold the axe like this—you see? Now, hold the wood with your left hand and come down with the axe on an angle! And *mind your hand!*"

The small axe bit hard into the length of tree limb, and I had to work it out.

"Now, again. And try to cut into the same place. Ah! Not bad, Deb. We'll make a woodsman of you yet!"

Or, another time, from Benjamin—"I'll race you, Deborah!"

"But I have all these skirts!"

"Never mind, just pick them up! Come on!"

"Ben—"

"Come on! You're just afraid I'll beat you!"

"I am not!"

"Then come *on!*"

And holding my skirts high I raced along the dirt track from the house to the barn, Benjamin thundering beside me, until I reached the goal two strides ahead of him.

"I won! I won!" I shouted triumphantly.

"You started ahead of me!"

"I did not! I can just run faster than you! If I only didn't have to bother with all these skirts! But I won!"

Both of us breathless, we collapsed on the grass, our backs against the warm barn wall, the sun on our faces. Ben's laughing brown eyes looked at me in mock solemnity and he shook his head.

"Deb, I vow you don't behave like any other female I ever knew! Ma told us we'd have to be gentle with you because you were a girl. She told us not to think we could treat you like another brother, because girls were different. She said you would probably rather knit, or sew, or maybe even play with a doll-baby if you had one." He stopped, looking at me closely. "Do you, Deb? Do you have a doll-baby?"

"No," I said. "I've never had one."

"Would you like one? I could make one for you—out of a corncob, maybe."

A doll-baby! Of my own! Something to play with and fondle—but I did not dare say yes. Wanting so much to please the boys, to be one of them, to *belong* to them, I felt I must do as they did, think as they thought. Giving up that precious doll-baby forever, I said, "I'd rather have my own gun."

Ben stared at me. "I vow you're a strange one! Not like a girl at all!"

"Oh, but I *can* be," I said anxiously. "I can be whatever you want me to be! I'll play with a doll-baby if you want me to—" Only please accept me, my heart cried. Please—take me in!

Ben laughed. "You don't have to change, Deb," he said. "You are all right as you are. Come on, I'll race you back again."

In addition to this new and wonderful acceptance into a young world, I was developing many domestic skills. If being "bound out" was not the horror I had feared, there were still hours each day spent working with Mrs. Thomas. Together we cooked the vast amounts of food it took to feed the family, we scrubbed their muddy footprints off the floors, we beat the dirt from their clothes with wooden paddles, sousing them up and down in the wash barrel.

And I learned to spin and to weave. The handling of the soft mounds of wool, sheared by the Deacon and his sons from the Thomas sheep, the gentle whir of the wheel, and the clacking of the shuttles on the loom became a passion with me. Mrs. Thomas was generous with her praise.

"I declare, Deborah, you have the touch for the wheel! You already handle it more quickly and smoothly than I do. We must find some beautiful dye, and use the very softest wool, and make a new frock for you."

"You mean *really* new? Just for *me?*"

"Of course! With only one girl in the family we must dress her as becomingly as we can."

I had owned only one new dress that I could remember, when I lived with Cousin Fuller. All the rest had been handed down, made over, taken up, or let out—but never new. And never meant just for me!

"I would be very careful of it, ma'am—I would wear it only on Sunday—for church meeting——"

"Dear child! It will be *your* dress! You will wear it whenever and wherever you please. A soft light blue, I think, to bring out the blue of your eyes. And your frock will come first. Those great hulks of boys must wait their turn."

The boys may have seemed "great hulks" to their mother, who stood about four feet and nine inches tall, the average height for a woman, but I was growing fast and already I was an inch taller than Benjamin, and almost three inches taller than Mrs. Thomas. It amused her when she had to look up to me.

"I cannot think what it is, Deborah—you're shooting up like a cornstalk!"

"It must be all the good things you feed us, and running with the boys, and—just being healthy and happy, I reckon, ma'am."

"You *are* happy here, aren't you, Deborah?"

"More than ever in my life!"

Except for Nathaniel and Jonathan, who were too old, the boys attended school fairly regularly during the winter when the demands of the farm lessened, and not infrequently I was sent along with them. Carrying hot baked potatoes to warm our hands (and later to eat cold for lunch) we would run, skip, and hop the two miles to the one-room schoolhouse. Sometimes we would see one of His Majesty's soldiers parading about in his colorful uniform, and the boys would find it impossible to resist the temptation of a snowball aimed at the proud tall hat.

"But you *mustn't,*" I would say, aghast at their effrontery. "He's an English soldier! He might shoot us!"

"Don't be a ninny, Deb! He wouldn't dare! He knows we'd tear him limb from limb!"

But I took no chances. I never threw a snowball myself.

I loved those days in school, and acquitted myself fairly well. I could read and do simple figuring, and I practiced my handwriting until it was neater than any scrawl the boys could produce. Robbie insisted it was not necessary to write "fancily" as long as it was legible, but I sometimes caught him practicing when he thought I didn't see.

And so the months went by, with season following season, and I felt myself a real part of the Thomas household. I was not treated as a servant, but as a daughter—one who naturally assisted in all domestic duties, but from custom, not from force. I was encouraged to play out-of-doors, and to help the boys with their farm chores, which I thoroughly enjoyed; I was taught to prepare the breads, the puddings, the little sweet tarts that the family liked, and commended when my efforts were properly light and tasty, and teased fraternally when they were not. I was given bright ribbons to be used in my caps or on my hair, and taught to roll that pale straight thatch around damp rags to curl the ends. My new dress filled me with pride (as I began to fill it with a slowly developing figure), and the very sight of its pale blue folds hanging from the wall peg in my room was enough to make me laugh aloud with joy.

"I feel so much at home here," I said one day to Mrs. Thomas. "As though I really *belonged!*"

"And so you do, Deborah. Not by birth, perhaps, but by affection." We were grinding dried herbs with mortar and pestle, and the tangy fragrance filled the kitchen. Mrs. Thomas did not look up as she added, "You never speak of your true home, child. Why not?"

My chin lifted. "I have no home save this. My mother rid herself of me years ago. Surely you know that."

"Fie, child! You speak as if it had been her choice!"

"Certainly it was not mine!"

"If she had not loved you so much, she would not have sent you away. Have you never thought of that?"

"But how can that be?"

"Deborah, your mother wanted more for you and her other children than she could give. She wanted you to be well-fed so you would grow strong. She wanted you to have proper clothing, and a healthy, guided up-bringing. When she sent you away it was an act of deep love, the most unselfish thing she could have done." She looked at me, her eyes serious. "Very often, Deb-orah, we have to give up the thing we love the most. You will learn that one day."

That gave me much to think on, and after that brief conversation I began to feel differently about my mother. Though I did not love her more, my bitterness toward her was less.

6 ☆ Blisters and Beans

It was in the spring following my thirteenth birthday in December that my lifelong interest in gardening began. I remember what a beautiful morning it was. I had been washing windows—sixteen little rectangular panes in each one—and seeing them sparkle as the sun came through. As I was polishing the last few panes Mrs. Thomas came into the room.

"How well you have cleaned them, Deborah! They shine! Now put the rags away and go outside and breathe the spring air. It's too beautiful a morning to spend indoors."

Once outside I could hear the boys' voices from way behind the barn where the fields lay, and I followed the sound. Phineas and Ben and Nathaniel and Jonathan were spading the ground for planting, and I stood and watched for a while. There was a rhythm to it—placing the edge of the spade carefully, pressing it down with a sturdy foot, lifting it out again, and turning the earth to fall into rich, dark mounds. I wanted to try and said so.

"This is man's work, Deb," Jonathan said. "You can pick the stuff when it's grown."

"Making things grow is everybody's work," I said firmly. "I want to dig."

Nathaniel straightened his back and looked at me disapprovingly. "Your hands will get all blistered, and then the blisters will turn into callouses, and then——"

"I don't *care!* Let me try!"

With a very superior grin Jonathan handed me his spade. "Very well, you stubborn wench, try. *You* dig, and *I'll* watch."

He settled himself on the ground, knees drawn up and his arms around them. "Well," he said, "go on."

I pressed the edge of the blade against the ground as I had watched the boys do, and set my foot on top, pushing down as hard as I could. I felt the solid earth give slightly as I worked the blade down into it. When it seemed deep enough I leaned back on the handle, raised the spadeful of dirt and watched with dismay as it slid off before I could turn it. Jonathan guffawed happily.

"Not as easy as it looks, is it?" he snickered.

"Maybe not," I said, "but I'll get it! Stop your silly cackling!"

Ben took pity on me. "You have to hold the spade as flat as you can when you bring it out," he said. "Press back with one hand and lift with the other."

That time I was more successful, but it was an hour or so later before I felt sure enough of my ability to stop. My hands were, indeed, blistered and sore, my back and legs ached unmercifully, my clothes clung to me from the perspiration, and I felt marvelous! I handed the spade back to Jonathan.

"Tomorrow I'll do more," I said graciously, "but now I shall allow you to dig." And before they could see how stiff I was I limped into the house.

Next morning my body ached so much I thought I could never crawl from my bed. I tried to give no indication of my wretched state as I helped Mistress Thomas serve breakfast, but all the boys were watching me and grinning. Of course Jonathan had to tell his father.

"Stubborn as a jenny mule she is," Jon said, "but it wasn't as easy as she thought it would be." He turned to me. "Come on, Deb, admit it. It wasn't easy, was it?"

"Things don't always have to be easy," I said with spirit. "I ache all over, I admit that, and my hands are sore, just as you said they would be. I admit that, too. But I should like to have a garden of my own! I'd spade it, and turn it, and plant it, and tend it—and I warrant I could grow better vegetables than you!"

Deacon Thomas laughed harder than I had ever heard him. "Shall we give her a chance to prove it, boys?" he asked. "I say we give Deborah her garden and let her take care of it. Whatever she raises is hers to do with as she will. Whether she puts it on our table or sells it to the neighbors is all one with me. And I shan't be at all surprised if what comes up in Deborah's patch is better than what the rest of us raise. You may as well admit something, too, sons. Our Deb is a match for you all!"

I stared at him. "May I truly have my own patch, Deacon Thomas? Do you mean it?"

"Certainly. Pick whatever spot you like and make it

as large as you can tend. There's plenty of land out there. But you are to do it all yourself. Is that understood?"

"Oh, yes, sir! Thank you!" I said. And then to those ten grinning faces, "And the rest of you—just wait!"

I recall that the household chores seemed endless that spring. There appeared to be no finish to the cooking, cleaning, and washing, the candle- and soap-making, the spinning, weaving, knitting, and sewing, the butter to be churned and the herbs to be dried, the eggs to be gathered and the chickens to be fed, the slops to be emptied and the woodbox to be filled—but when, at last, such things were done, I spent all my time working in my garden.

My hands, as Nat had promised, grew calloused, and my nails seemed never to be clean, but my muscles hardened so my back no longer ached, and when the first tiny shoots broke through the ground all my efforts were repaid. I don't know where I first heard the Indian advice that corn should not be planted until the leaves on the oak trees were the size of a mouse's ear, but I heeded it (which the boys did not) and my corn grew in beautiful straight rows, strong and tall. My beans climbed neatly up the tripods I built for them, my root vegetables sent up their green signals, my peas grew plump and sweet.

One evening Robbie sprawled comfortably on the ground watching me work. He had offered to help and I had refused.

"No, this is all mine! I never had a garden before,

and I want to be able to say I did it all myself. Just sit and talk to me."

That was when Robbie stretched out, his long legs getting in my way, but I would never have told him.

"I don't know why it is," he said, "but even your squash stays where you want it to. Ours goes helter-skeltering all over the place."

"My squash wouldn't *dare* to stray," I said sternly. "It knows I'd be after it in a minute with the sharp edge of the hoe!"

"Determined Deb," Rob teased in his newly deepened voice. "You never intend to let anyone get ahead of you, do you?"

Suddenly serious, I dropped my hoe and slipped to my knees beside him. "Oh, Robbie, does it seem like that? I never mean it to! It is only that—well, I—*admire* you all so much! I want to do the things you do! I want you to be—*proud* of me! I don't want to be left out just because I am a girl!"

Rob laughed. "The next thing we know you will be stramming about in our cast-off breeches and trying to grow a beard!"

I lifted my hand to pummel him in mock anger, but he caught both my arms and forced me back onto the ground, still laughing. "Someone is going to have to teach you your place," he said. "You're getting much too uppity!"

His face was just inches from mine, and I watched his eyes change from laughter to . . . something I could not name. We did not move, and my heart began to pound in a way it never had before. Rob's strong hands trembled as they held my wrists. Then suddenly he released me and jumped to his feet. When he spoke, his voice was husky, as if his mouth were dry.

"Get on with your gardening, girl. Already you make the rest of us farmers look like horse traders. Your little plot outstrips ours by far!"

And to my bewilderment he turned and walked quickly away, stumbling once in his haste. It was some minutes before my heart stopped thumping.

7 ☆ The First Gun

When I saw the damage done to my precious garden by an army of hungry marauding rabbits I boiled!

"I'll kill them!" I exploded. "I'll kill every one of them! Nathaniel, may I borrow your gun?"

"No, ma'am!" said Nat flatly.

"Please? Just until I get those long-eared thieves?"

"Did you ever shoot a gun, Deb?"

"No, but—"

"It would kick you backwards off the acres!"

"Does it kick *you* backwards?"

"Not now, but it did when I first tried it, when I was about your age."

"If you could learn to shoot it, so can I! You just hold it up, point it and pull something, don't you?"

The older boys looked at each other with resignation, and Robbie sighed.

"She's going to learn to shoot, so we may as well teach her not to shoot herself. I'll put up some sort of target way down behind the barn. Somebody bring a gun. Come along, Deb."

Mistress Thomas watched us from the doorway as we started across the fields.

"Boys, you watch out for her, now! If Deborah gets hurt—"

"She won't, Ma. We'll teach her to be careful. Don't fret."

They were as good as their word. While Robbie fastened a piece of white cloth to the broadest tree trunk he could find, Nat showed me how to pour a charge of powder down the long barrel of his rifle. He then centered a patch of greased cloth over the open end—"That's the bore of the gun. Watch out for it!"—and placed a lead ball on it, ramming them home with the long iron rod.

"Now, Deb, stand back here."

"But that's so far away!"

"Not far at all. Stand here, where I told you."

The target looked at least a mile away, though it may not have been more than a hundred yards. (Later I learned from experience that three hundred yards is not too far for a good rifleman to score a perfect hit.) And so, surrounded by my advisors, I made my first shot and they gallantly caught me when I came close to being knocked on my backside.

If they laughed themselves sick when I repeatedly missed the target and gouged great scars in the broad tree trunk, I could not blame them, though I fumed. Nor would I stop before I had landed my shot on the white target at least once. When I achieved that they all cheered lustily, and I was loudest of all. After that first session I could think of nothing more than the ache in my shoulder from the recoil of the gun, the ringing in my ears from the report, and the strange excitement I had felt when it was Rob's strong hands that caught me.

Whenever there was time to spare some of the boys would take me out to the farthest acres—"We have to protect the neighbors, Deb!"—and show me repeatedly how to load, how to brace myself, and how to aim. Their teaching was successful, for one early morning two or three weeks later, when the dew was still cool and wet on the high grass, I walked through the fields to the house, the rifle over my shoulder and my booty in my hand.

Mrs. Thomas was just stirring the breakfast porridge and the boys were on their way to the barn for the morning chores when I appeared in the doorway.

"Deborah!" Mrs. Thomas said. "I thought you were still abed. Are you all right? I fancied I heard gunshots a while back, but then I felt I must have been mistaken."

Ephraim looked at what I was carrying. "You heard them all right, Ma. Deb's been out protecting her farm patch, I figure."

Proudly I held the two limp rabbits up by their ears. "There's two less for me to fret about, and I scared a lot more from here to Kingdom Come. If somebody will teach me how to skin them I think I'll make me a fur cap. And we can have rabbit stew for supper tonight."

Ephraim rubbed his stomach, rolling his eyes up. "My favorite dish! Rabbit stew with a scattering of rifle shot in it!"

I threw the rabbits to him. "You don't have to eat

any," I said. "Just show me how to skin these things!"

The rabbit stew was seasoned by the conversation at the table.

"The English are just getting too high and mighty in their ways," Nathaniel complained. "You'd think those soldiers were invited guests here! I met with one in Sproat's Tavern today. He appeared to feel his second tankard of ale should be a gift!"

"There seem to be more of them all the time," Jon added. "King George must consider us a dangerous people from the number of troops he sends here."

"The poor lonely men," Mistress Thomas murmured. "Such a distance from home, and without their families."

"That situation could be easily repaired," said Nat. "Let the poor lonely men go home again! We can manage quite nicely without their supervision!"

Deacon Thomas's voice held a note of warning. "Do not speak carelessly, Nat. I am sure you are aware of a certain unrest hereabouts. It would not be wise to cause hard feelings."

"The hard feelings already exist, Father. But I will try not to add to them. However, it will not be easy. My dislike for those beautiful scarlet coats increases daily!"

So much for the rabbit stew. With Mrs. Thomas's aid, the fur was made into a most fetching bonnet, in which I quite admired myself. I noted that Robbie liked it, too.

8 ☆ The First News of War

In early December, 1774, shortly before my fourteenth birthday on the seventeenth day of the month, dear Reverend Conant came calling late one afternoon. Mistress Thomas asked him to sup with us, and while I was helping her serve the meal he told me how well I looked, and I thanked him.

"And dear me, how you've grown, Deborah! Where's that pale-haired, big-eyed little mouse I brought here four years ago?"

"That little mouse has turned into a fearsome, axe-wielding, rabbit-hunting female," said Phineas. "She is determined that anything we can do she can do just as well—and privately she feels she is better."

I thrust the bowl of beaten potatoes so near his face that he came close to getting his nose in it.

"Will you have some, Phinny?" I asked sweetly, and then whispered, "And fill your mouth as you usually do so you can't talk so much!"

But it was impossible to keep all ten of them quiet, and it was Jonathan who spoke up next.

"We have decided that the only way we can rid ourselves of her is to marry her off," he said, "but we can't find anyone brave enough. We have been considering one of those high-nosed British soldiers—what would you think of that, Reverend?"

Sylvanus Conant smiled. "I think that the day Deborah leaves this house all ten of you boys will be weeping like babes. That is what I think. But whatever you do, don't wed her to a British soldier. England is not in high favor with the colonies these days, you know."

"I have heard the rumblings from Boston-way," Deacon Thomas said. "Do they amount to anything?"

"Yes, I think they do. I am sure you know that there has been a general agreement between all the colonies, from New Hampshire to South Carolina, on a group of pledges designed to give us more independence from England. As I understand it, old George the Third seems to pay little attention to any requests we have made so far concerning laws and rules and taxes, and there are those who feel it may be time for something stronger than requests."

"Such as what?"

"Demands, mayhap, or even—action."

His attention fortunately diverted from me, Jonathan spoke. "Action? What sort of action? You mean *fighting?*"

"I sincerely trust not," Reverend Conant said quickly. "But if that British general, Thomas Gage, doesn't move some of his troops away from Boston I fear some hot-headed colonial may make a foolish mistake. Feelings are high around the city. It would take very little to light a fire."

And not more than a few months later the fire was

lit. It was a cool April evening, and I was sowing a few more rows in my second spring's garden, when Samuel came hurtling down the fields to where I worked.

"Deb! Deb! Come up to the hou-hou-house," he stammered. "Nathaniel a-a-and Jon just got back fr-fr-from town and they have big n-n-n-news!"

Hunkered down, my hand full of seeds, I looked at him over my shoulder. "What sort of news? Can it not wait till I finish these rows?"

"No! Come n-n-now! Come on, I'll ra-ra-race you!"

And since that was an invitation I could not resist, I poured the seeds into my pocket, lifted my skirts in two hands, and headed for the house. Samuel won, though not by very much, and we were both flushed and panting when we entered the kitchen. Nat and Jon were talking as fast as they could, interrupting each other and tripping over their words.

"There were two particular men General Gage was after, I heard," Nat was saying, "one named Adams, I forget the first name——"

"Samuel," Jonathan contributed. "Samuel Adams and John Hancock."

"That's right," Nat went on. "It seems Gage knew those two were sitting on a great store of guns and ammunition and so on, in Concord, north of Boston about twenty miles——"

Jonathan took over the story. "So Gage sent about seven hundred men to capture Adams and Hancock and destroy the supplies, but there were three other men—one was a William Dawes and another a Dr. Prescott, and the third one was—was——"

"Paul Revere," said Nat, "and those three learned of Gage's troops marching on Lexington——"

"But you said Concord before," I interrupted, confused.

"The supplies were in Concord, but Adams and Hancock were in Lexington, just a few miles away," Jonathan explained. "Now, will you let me tell it?"

"Go on," I said.

"So those three, Paul Revere and Dawes and Prescott, jumped into their saddles and off they went—oh, I wish I had been there!—and they alerted everyone for miles around that the Redcoats were on the way. And when Gage's men appeared in Lexington at dawn——"

Nathaniel could be silent no longer. "What was the first thing they saw but a lot of the village men, about forty of them, all lined up with their rifles aimed! There was a real skirmish, not big enough to be called a battle, I reckon, but eight of our men were killed and nine more were wounded before the British troops went on to Concord."

"Oh dear," sighed Mistress Thomas. "Killed! And wounded!"

"And that is not all," Nathaniel rushed on before Jonathan could speak, "the British reached Concord and destroyed the supplies, but they had to fight off another attack at some bridge—the old North Bridge, I recollect it was—and they lost fourteen men! Then they started back to their camp at Charlestown, but from all around the Concord area farmers grabbed their rifles and took off after the Redcoats. They hid in trees and behind fences and anywhere they could, and they picked off those bloodybacks one after another!"

"Nathaniel!" said a shocked Mrs. Thomas.

"But that's what folk call them, Ma," Jonathan broke in. "Gage's men must have sent for help, because more than a thousand reinforcements arrived—a thousand!—and there was a right sharp bit of fighting going on. The blo—I mean the *Englishmen*—made it back to Charlestown, but it is said they lost close to two hundred and fifty men, and *we* lost only eighty-eight!"

"*Only* eighty-eight," breathed Mrs. Thomas. "Eighty-eight good men dead!"

"Old General Gage is going to think twice before he tries his little tricks again," Nat said with relish. "The colonists are not such fumbling boobies as he may have thought!"

"But what is to happen now, I wonder?" murmured Deacon Thomas.

"No one we talked to seems to know, but I think we can be sure it is the start of something. After that bloodletting those farmers are not going to settle back picking beans again. They don't want the British interfering and they have told them so, with guns. If those Englishmen are as smart as they claim to be they'll take heed! Massachusetts men are not to be dictated to!"

There was a little silence in the room, and then Mrs. Thomas got to her feet with a sigh. "Well, whatever comes, there are still the evening chores to do," she said. "Ben, have all the cows been milked? Jeremiah, fill the kindling box for me, please. Nat, did you bring back the molasses and salt that I sent you for? Fetch them in so Deborah can put them away. I want to get my thoughts on homely things! I cannot think of war!"

And that was the first real word of all that was to come.

9 ☆ Drilling on the Green

Looking back, I can see how events were building into a pattern that could develop in only one way, although I know now that way was not at first intended. What had begun as resistance to inequalities was now a determined refusal to accept oppression.

Although the very existence of the Second Continental Congress had been declared unlawful by the British governing authorities stationed in America, and although it had been strictly forbidden to meet, meet it did in May of '75, in Philadelphia. The Lexington-Concord affair had enraged all the colonies, and the delegates to Congress made it evident that they would support Massachusetts to the hilt. The word *independence* was not mentioned, but a declaration listing "the Causes and Necessities of Taking Up Arms" stated that "Our Cause is just. Our Union is perfect. Our internal resources are great. . . ." As Robbie said thoughtfully, "If those words do not spell *independence* then nothing does!"

Everyone felt the unrest. After church meetings, on village streets, in farmyards and taverns, men talked together, debating their own views on breaking with

England. Small military companies were formed and in every town men drilled on the village greens. With officers elected from among themselves, there they stood after the evening chores were done, trying to look like soldiers. Their familiar guns, used always to hunt game, not men, they tried to handle in a military manner. It somehow both saddened and thrilled me.

James, David, and Jeremiah were too young, since only those of sixteen or older were permitted to join these companies, but the seven eldest boys raced through their farm work on drilling nights, and sped to join their fellows, filled with pride and excitement. When Nat was made a lieutenant he took to muttering orders under his breath as he went about his work.

"Shoulder—arms!" he would murmur as he carried spade or hoe into the fields. "Atten-tion!" as he pushed a cow into position for milking. "Company—march!" as he pursued a hen whose destiny was to be that day's dinner. We teased him, but he was—as Nathaniel always was—totally serious.

"This is not a game, Deb! This is soldiering!"

Sometimes I would go with the Thomas boys and watch them as they lined up with the other townsmen for practice. What a motley crew they were! Tall and short, fat and thin, young and old, dressed any which way, and carrying whatever weapon they could get their hands on. Virtually the only requirement for military duty that I could see was two teeth that met to bite the top from a cartridge. But they were serious. We all were. The time had come when we viewed the prospect of war with acceptance. It was only Robbie who seemed less enthusiastic about the drilling, and who rarely chose to talk of a possible war.

It was about then that the Continental Army was formed, and a man named George Washington, a Virginian, was placed at its head. Unfortunately, he was nowhere near Boston in June, when his presence might have made a remarkable difference.

It took some time for word of what was happening to reach us, and when it did come it was so often exaggerated that we learned not to be too credulous. But there was little doubt about the affair at Breed's Hill (which somehow, in later reports, was mistakenly called Bunker Hill), and it affected us all in varying ways as we sat discussing it at the supper table.

Jeremiah, a husky thirteen-year-old, would have liked nothing better than single-handed combat with British General Gage.

"I'd get him just the way Deb gets rabbits!" he said fiercely. "Why does he want to fight us anyhow, Pa?"

"I don't think he intended to," the Deacon said. "He simply meant to strengthen the position of his troops around Boston in case of trouble."

"And he got it," said Jeremiah with satisfaction, "from all those men on Breed's Hill!"

"But those men were routed, Jerry," his father pointed out. "Our men did not win that battle."

It was Samuel who broke in, stammering as he always did when excited. "How-how-how could we? The British fired on us from those great wa-wa-warships in Boston Harbor!"

"We drove them off twice, Sam," Jeremiah told him,

"and we killed a lot of them! We'd have killed even more if our powder hadn't run out, and if we'd had bayonets!"

"I wish we did not have to talk about killing." That was Mistress Thomas's soft voice. "Why must there be killing?"

"Because the British won't listen to us when we talk, Ma," Phineas told her. "It is the British who have stationed soldiers all over our country. They are the ones who began all this."

"But we are a British colony," I said. Jerry interrupted.

"Why should we be? We are a young, strong nation. We don't need England and Lord North and King George to tell us what to do! We have built this country ourselves—we should run it ourselves!"

My mind flashed to the verse my mother had written. "John Alden, Miles Standish, helped settle this land, and Governor Bradford ruled well that small band." My people. My land. Suddenly I felt a hot indignation against Great Britain and its desire to control us.

"I wish I were a man," I said stoutly. "I would be a militiaman and fight Gage and all his soldiers, and *we'd win!*"

Solemn Nathaniel looked at me, but there was a laugh deep in his dark eyes. "Mayhap that is what we should do—send Deborah, armed with her rabbit-rifle, off to meet with General Gage. I doubt not that she would come marching home carrying the General by the ears."

"And so I would," I said.

The month after the battle at Breed's Hill General Washington arrived in Cambridge, Massachusetts, ready for active duty. He was met by some sixteen thousand men, rowdy, only half-trained if they were trained at all, dressed in whatever garments they happened to possess. A raggle-taggle army that broke into cheers for the tall, dignified, serious man who rode up to them. In that enthusiastic, burning crew were Nat and Jonathan and Phineas.

They enlisted first and told us about it later, all very proud of themselves, but concerned as to how their news might be received. It came as no surprise to their parents or to me. With the air so filled with patriotism and brave slogans it had been only a matter of time before the Thomas boys joined up.

And off they marched. Robbie became more quiet than ever, but Ben, Ephraim, Sam, the twins, and Jeremiah were envious and dejected.

"Some of you must stay here to keep the place going," the Deacon reminded them. "Not just for ourselves, but because the need for food will be great. It is as much a duty as fighting, boys."

"But not the same," Ben muttered. "Nothing like the same."

Word came back to us that they had been sent to New York with the troops who were trying to hold the city against General Howe. We heard stories of the months of advances and retreats, the small battles won and lost. As the Confederates were forced back into New Jersey and then into Pennsylvania, the deserters started coming home with tales of cold and hunger and slaughter which they no longer chose to be a part of. That, I think, was what determined Ben to go.

"They are running like rats," he said angrily. "Do they think they can fight a war in cozy, comfortable warmth? With no wounds and no deaths? With fat bellies and downy beds? Washington started with almost twenty thousand men. Now I hear there are not more than three thousand! And most of that loss is from desertions! I am going. I have to!"

"And I am going with you," Ephraim said.

"No, Eph. Not now. Later, if you must, but not two of us at once. It might be more than Father could accept now. He is not well."

"You think Ma is stronger?"

"In many ways, yes. Women are born so. Look at Deb! *She* won't weep for me—will you, Deb?"

And I thought to myself, yes. I will. For you and all the young men. But I will not weep openly, because you *want* to go. "If I weep for you, Ben," I said, "I will not tax you with it. And Ben is right, Eph. You must not go, not yet."

And so, surly-faced and fuming, Ephraim stood with me and waved after Benjamin when he left. Dear Ben, with whom I had first raced along the track to the barn, who had offered to make me a corncob doll-baby. Ben, grown up and gone off soldiering.

10 ☆ Robbie

Rural life has its own demanding cycle, and there were weeks at a time when all our attention was concentrated on the daily routine, with little thought to spare for larger events. Ephraim, Robbie, and Sam were bearing the tremendous task of keeping our many acres of farmland producing as much as they could, for Deacon Thomas was now in poor health and unable to assist them. At fairly regular intervals a wagon driven by a soldier would arrive to carry away bushels of whatever crops were in season, occasionally giving us money in payment, but more often simply a paper saying money was due.

One fall day such a driver arrived, and while Jamie, Dave, and Jerry loaded his wagon, he sat with us in the farm kitchen. Mistress Thomas and I were knitting woolen hose and caps and mufflers for the coming winter, the Deacon sat quietly on the settle by the fire, and Eph, Robbie, and Sam straddled the rush-bottomed chairs, listening avidly. The sun, coming in through the small-paned window, shone on Robbie's thick hair and made it gleam like gold.

"They have burned Falmouth," the soldier said. "I hear tell there is nothing left of it."

"Falmouth?" Eph asked. "Where is Falmouth?"

"In Maine. The British burned it to the ground."

Eph's face slowly turned a deep red with anger. "For no reason? They burned a town for no reason?"

"For the reason that it was a coast town and therefore a threat. It now makes an excellent landing place for the British navy."

Deliberately Ephraim got to his feet, his hands gripping the back of the chair so tightly the knuckles showed white. "I am going, Father," he said. "I know—" as the Deacon raised a hand in protest, "I know you don't want me to, but I must. The younger boys can work the farm, with Rob and Sam to guide them, but I can sit here no longer. To destroy a *town*! I am sorry, Ma, I am *sorry*! But I have to go!"

And Mistress Thomas took her husband's hand without looking at him and said quietly to Ephraim, "Yes, son. I know you do."

And Ephraim left us.

The busy spring and summer came, and events on the farm and in the world at large increased in urgency. Robbie refused to let any of the acres lie fallow, and drove himself and the four younger boys until at night they could barely stay awake long enough to eat their supper before falling into bed. As often as I could I worked beside him, trying to lighten his chores a little, trying to bring back the bright smile that had been so much a part of Robbie, and which now we rarely saw.

One morning I walked down through the fields carrying a pitcher of buttermilk, chilled from the spring house.

"Sit down, Robbie. Drink a little."

"No time, Deb. There is so much to do."

"You will work all the better for a few minutes' rest. Come now."

He looked ready to argue again, but then, with a ghost of the old grin, he let himself down to the ground. I edged as close to him as I could. More and more I wanted to *touch* Rob, wanted to feel his hands on me. Perhaps because there had been so few caresses in my life I needed the physical evidences of affection. I knew in my mind that Robbie liked me. I needed to know it through my body also. Now I knelt beside him, my brown work dress inches from his cheek.

"I never knew so much of me could ache all at once," he said softly, and took a long drink of the cool milk. "Ah, Deb, that's good!" He stretched out, propping his head on his hand, and looked at me. "How do you always know what I need?"

"Because I know you," I said. "You would force yourself to work until you staggered if you were not halted sometimes."

He turned over onto his stomach, burying his face in his folded arms. His voice was muffled.

"Oh, Deb—don't you see why I work this hard? Because I don't dare to think about the fighting! That is what I *should* be doing—and I can't bear the thought of it! I am a coward, Deb! A coward!"

I let my hand reach out and smooth his shining hair. It felt warm and damp from the sun.

"No, Robbie! That is not true! You are no coward—you know within yourself that you are not! I won't let you say it!"

"But it *is* true, Deb! Nat, Jon, Phinny, Ben, Eph—all of them went as soon as they felt they should. They are all in the thick of it—fighting my war for me! *They* were not afraid to go!"

"It isn't fear, Robbie. It is just that you are different from the others. You have always been. Gentler, quieter, kinder—not to like bloodshed does not make a coward! And I don't suppose all the others looked forward to war."

"But they *went!* Don't you see? That is the difference! Whether they wanted to go or not, they *did* go! And I—I just stay here, playing in the dirt!"

"What you are doing is not playing! *Someone* has to raise food. Who is going to feed all those men? Robbie, shake some sense into your head! There are *different* ways of serving one's country—not just *one* way!"

There was silence for a moment. My heart ached for him. Presently he turned over and lay on his back, one arm shielding his eyes from the sun.

"Come closer, Deb. I need to feel you close."

I shifted so that I lay beside him, my head pillowed on his shoulder, my arm across his chest. After a moment he pulled me roughly, quickly against him, so that I could feel the solid hardness of his body the full length of mine, and it was as though we could not get close enough to each other. My hand could feel the rapid beating of his heart, and Rob's fingers curved and pressed around my breast. It seemed as if my whole body were beating with the same breathless, shaking rhythm as his. He turned his head slowly until he could see my face, and then somehow we lay breast to chest, belly to belly, loins to loins and I was filled with a liquid fire and I could barely breathe. His lips found mine, and as we kissed we moved again until I lay stretched on my back amid the tall grass, supporting his weight and pulling him close against me. His mouth left mine, only to cover my cheeks, my eyelids, my forehead with quick hard kisses.

"Oh, Deborah!" His voice was no more than a breath. "I love you so!"

"And I love you, Rob! Always and always I love you!"

"How can you love a coward, Deb? A man who won't even do his own fighting?"

"I don't *want* you to fight! You must not leave me, Robbie—please, *please* don't leave me!"

And again we kissed until my lips were bruised, and his hands caressed my body through my rumpled dress, and when at last he would have moved away from me I clasped him close and held him with all my strength.

"I can't let you go, Rob!"

"I must—while I still can!" He sat up, taking my hands and pulling me so that I sat straight beside him. My cap lay crushed on the grass, my hair fell loose and disordered. "My beautiful Deborah," he said, and smoothed my hair back from my face.

And then he stood and lifted me to my feet, and with our arms around each other we kissed again, and the touch of our bodies took the place of words. When at last he pushed me gently away from him and held me at arm's length a moment, looking deep into my eyes before bending to pick up his spade, I walked slowly backwards up the fields so that I need not take my eyes from him. And my heart still pounded, and my knees trembled, and I was filled with a fierce hunger I had never known before. The physical closeness I had wanted so much had not satisfied me, it had awakened me!

All life was suddenly changed because Robbie and I were in love. I flew through each day's tasks so I could be with him in the fields, or the barns, or the pasture, or wherever he might be. I primped and fussed with my appearance, leaving off my housecap at times to tie ribbons in my hair, choosing carefully from among my several frocks, arranging the ruffles of sleeve or fichu until they fell just so, pinching my cheeks to bring more color to my face—although that, as Mistress Thomas pointed out with loving amusement, was hardly necessary.

"You glow like a taper, Deborah dear! I vow there is no need for candles when you are in the room."

I swirled around, my skirts billowing about me, and then leaned and kissed the woman's cheek.

"I am so happy I think I cannot bear it," I told her.

"And the Deacon and I are happy for you, child. For you and Rob both. Nothing could please us more."

Rob and I had not spoken of marriage; there was no need. Of *course* we would marry. Nor did we speak of his enlisting. I hoped with all my heart that our discovery of this wonderful love would keep him by me. Surely the outcome of the war—which was not yet truly termed a *war*—would not be changed by what Robert Thomas might do. One reluctant young soldier could not alter the pattern of history.

And so we talked of love during those early summer months of 1776, and we kissed and held each other close, and laughed together, and sometimes found our emotions so overpowering it was all we could do to step apart. I had never suspected I could be so filled with passion! Rob was stronger—or more prudent—than I.

"Someday soon, Deb. Soon! When we can be always together!"

And we kissed again, more gently, and the world was sweet.

It was about that time that Sam enlisted. He could not wait to be on his way. Robbie held my hand tightly as we watched Sam close the gate behind him and start jauntily down the road.

"I am going to have to go, Deb. I cannot let my brothers save my country for me much longer."

And I put both arms around his waist and held him close. "Not yet, Robbie," I begged. "Not yet. Don't leave me—not yet!"

11 ☆ Nat

Later that summer of 1776, we sat in church on a warm, fragrant Sabbath, and heard Reverend Conant read a declaration. The words he spoke were being read to Americans in every church, in every meeting-house, on every village green, and I sat between Mistress Thomas and Robbie and listened to them.

"When in the Course of human Events, it becomes necessary for one People to dissolve the Political Bands which have connected them with another, and to assume among the Powers of the Earth, the separate and equal Station to which the Laws of Nature and of Nature's God entitle them, a decent Respect to the Opinions of Mankind requires that they should declare the causes which impel them to the Separation."

And I thought, now America has spoken! Now what we feel is being made known, not only to each one of us who helped make this country, but also to those who would unfairly possess it.

Reverend Conant's firm voice went on, and my whole body thrilled. "We hold these Truths to be self-evident, that all Men are created equal, that they are endowed by their Creator with certain unalienable

Rights, that among these are Life, Liberty, and the pursuit of Happiness." I turned to look at Robbie, and his blue eyes met mine with an intensity that frightened me.

The declaration ended with a list of the names of men who had promised to support it with, as the Reverend Conant read, "a firm Reliance on the Protection of Divine Providence," and who mutually pledged "to each other our Lives, our Fortunes, and our sacred honor."

The church emptied almost silently, and almost silently we walked home, my hand clasped tight in Rob's.

There was a horse tied to the hitching rail outside the Thomases' house, and a tall, dark-haired young man lounged against the fence. A nice-looking man, with a face that seemed made for smiling, but was now sober. He straightened up as we came through the gate.

"Deacon Thomas?" he asked.

"I am Deacon Thomas. How can I help you?"

The man touched the brim of a disreputable hat. "A message for you, sir." From inside his jacket he took a folded, sealed paper, and handed it to the Deacon. Deacon Thomas stood holding it, looking at it without breaking the seal.

How does one know certain things? I knew what news the message held, I simply did not know which boy.

The man who had brought it looked at each of us, and his dark eyes, serious and gentle, seemed to linger an extra moment on my face, and then dropped to where Rob's hand and mine were linked. He cleared his throat before he spoke again, but even so his voice was gruff.

"I was riding this way, I was asked to deliver it." He turned, unhitched the horse, and put one foot in the stirrup, and then added, "I am truly sorry." Mounting, he guided the horse back onto the road and disappeared.

Nathaniel had been killed.

When I saw Rob ride into the farmyard from the direction of the village a few days later I knew where he had been, and I thought I could not stand it.

"I have joined the army, Deb."

"Yes, Robbie. I know."

He took my hand and we walked slowly down the fields. The sun felt warm on our heads, and the soft, scented summer breeze stirred the tall grass, and shivered my world around me.

"I still loathe the thought of war, but now it is something I *must* do. For Nat—for you—for myself. For this land that I love so much. If I could just stay on here—with the fields, and the calm, quiet days, and the feel of the earth and of you in my arms—but to *have* these things I must *earn* them! Do you understand?"

"Understand? No, Rob, I do *not* understand! You don't *want* to go, no one has told you that you *ought* to go—Rob, we have just found each other! How can you think of going away now? And in any case, what difference would it make? If there is to be a war, then there *will* be, with or without you! And whether we win or lose it—what effect could you have on that? Oh, Robbie—darling Robbie—don't talk of it anymore!"

"But I must. Not only talk of it, but *do* it! Deborah, I love you. I want to live in peace with you always. And I never want to feel shame for myself! I could take the very easy way—stay with you here, telling myself what you have told me, that one man—that *I*—can make no difference. But it makes a difference to *me!* There are some things a man must do for his . . . conscience, perhaps, or his honor, whatever you choose to call it, else he is no man. And I will not offer you less than a man, Deb."

"But, Robbie . . ."

"Hush!" He stopped my words with a kiss, holding me tight. "Nothing you can say will change me, love. I am not sure myself whether this thing that I am about to do is for you, or for Nat, or for me. I only know it must be done. Make it easier for me, Deborah, not harder."

And we stood clasped close together, and my tears wet the shoulder of his homespun shirt, and I was half-past fifteen and Robbie was nearly eighteen, and I loved him so I thought my heart would break.

And Robbie went to war, and that was our good-bye.

As our small, lonely world settled into the routine of a country at war we became used to many things. With so few hands to work the farm, most of it was allowed to go back to fields. The number of sheep and cattle and other livestock dwindled. We could no longer care for them. We lost our amazement at seeing helmeted Hessian soldiers, those German mercenaries hired by the British to fight in place of the many Englishmen whose sympathies were with the colonists. And we were no longer surprised when David and James enlisted the moment they became sixteen. Jeremiah, the youngest, the baby, did not even wait that long. He took himself off, lied about his age, and at fifteen years old was a Continental soldier.

In a matter of days after Jerry left, the Deacon and Mrs. Thomas seemed like old, old people. There was little I could do to comfort them.

The farmhouse was so quiet!

We were avid for any scrap of news that we could gather. Nowadays, as I write this, newspapers are an accepted part of daily life, but there were no newspapers in the village of Middleborough in 1777. Our knowledge of events came by word of mouth.

We heard the story of Brandywine Creek from a soldier who had lost an arm there. He was trudging home, of little use now to the army, and when he passed our farm Mistress Thomas called him in. We fed him and he told us of the crushing defeat Washington's men had suffered. I have never heard the name of Brandywine Creek since without imagining it running red with the blood of that young man and the many others like him.

The next defeat was also in Pennsylvania at a place called Germantown. We were told of that by Reverend Conant. That was the last time I saw that kind man. He died in December of the smallpox. He was fifty-eight years old then, and had spent thirty-three of those years administering the gospel. He had been my good friend, and I missed him sorely. I could not go back to the First Congregational Church after that—he was so very much a part of that meetinghouse it seemed empty without him.

But just before the Reverend died we heard with joy of a great victory at Saratoga, New York, where General Horatio Gates achieved the surrender of the British general, Burgoyne. It put new heart into all of us, strengthened even further by the news that the French were about to join our forces against the British. Even as lonely as the three of us were—the Deacon, Mrs. Thomas, and I—we could not help but feel hope that the tide had turned and perhaps the boys would be coming home again soon.

Except for Nat.

12 ☆ Deborah Unbound

There had been a time, only a few years ago, when I had wondered what I would do when I became eighteen and was no longer bound to the Thomases, but I had never formed a plan. Then, of course, had come the shining discovery of Rob's and my love for each other, and I had thought of nothing but our marriage. It seemed only natural to stay on in the house that had become my home until Robbie could come back to me.

The December came that held my eighteenth birthday—1778—and marriage was no closer. It seemed so long since Rob had gone! I was frightened sometimes because I could not recall his face clearly, though I could always see the bright gleam of his hair and hear his quiet voice. I felt restless, and lonely, and dissatisfied—and empty. The farm and household chores had dwindled to a scant few, and the energy that has always filled me seemed never to be expended. I prowled the house, looking for something to keep me occupied. I slept poorly, and my usual hearty appetite diminished until I no more than picked at my food. I desperately needed to be *used*. Mrs. Thomas's knowledge of me, based on her deep and real affection, caused her to search for a solution. She came to me one frosty February morning, a smile on her sweet, aging face.

"Deborah dear, Benjamin Leonard's wife—you know her?" I nodded. I had seen her in church every week when Reverend Conant was there, and had talked with her often. "She asked me if I thought you would do some spinning and weaving for her. She admires your work, and her hands are very crippled in this cold weather. Would you be willing?"

Eagerly I grasped at some change in the routine, at a chance to keep myself busy. I moved to Barden Hills, not more than two miles from the farmhouse, and spent weeks there, soothed by the work I had always liked the most. The Leonards' house was warm and snug that freezing winter, and as I busied my hands with the quiet work I talked with Jennie, the lovely young Negro servant girl. She was a gay and laughing person, and as we spoke of our lives, and of the war, and of the men we each loved, we became close friends.

After some time with the Leonards I went to other houses where I did the same quiet spinning and weaving, and sometimes sewing, for different neighbors, and between times I went back to my little room at the Thomases'. And the months of the year slid slowly round and it seemed that Rob had been gone forever. The face I looked at in my wavery little mirror had changed. Had Rob changed too?

In the early winter of 1779 I was asked to teach at one of the small schools near Middleborough. The previous schoolmaster had gone to war, and a new teacher was needed. Happily I accepted! I was not sure whether I would be much more advanced than my pupils, but it was something to do—it was a *need* for me. Early each morning I left the Thomas house and walked the few miles over the hard-frozen dirt roads, or crunched through snow, and it made me remember the years when I had hopped, skipped, and jumped my way to school with the boys. My step was longer now, and less flighty, but sometimes I still carried that hot baked potato to warm my hands and to remind me of those less lonely times.

Blessings on dear Sylvanus Conant for the books he had given me so long ago! The little schoolhouse had few, all of which the older students knew by heart, and mine brought something new and exciting into their lives. To fill my days, I filled theirs. I taught them to read, to spell, and to do such simple figuring as I could manage myself. I devoted time to their penmanship, smiling as I recalled Robbie saying writing didn't have to be "fancy" as long as it was legible. I helped the girls with their knitting, and guided their stitches as they tried samplers. I showed the little boys how to throw a ball that traveled hard and straight and fast (thereby earning admiration from even the older lads), taught them to play mumblety-peg with a knife, and how to tie different kinds of knots in a piece of rope. Everything I had learned from the Thomas boys now stood me in good stead. As for maintaining discipline, I had no trouble. Even the sturdiest and most mischievous boys were awed by a female teacher who towered above them.

From time to time we had news of the Thomas boys,

usually brought by some soldier returning home after having been wounded. Very rarely were there letters —the lads had always been better with spades than quills—but one day when I was walking back to the Thomas house after a day of schoolteaching I saw a horse and rider trotting briskly toward me. There was something familiar about the man that I could not quite place. He reined up and touched a hand to his battered hat.

"You are Mistress Deborah Sampson?" he asked. His breath came out as white vapor in the cold air. I assented, and he went on. "I have a letter for you."

"For *me?*"

"Aye. From a Corporal Robert Thomas."

My knees felt suddenly weak. "Robbie! He is not——"

The tall man grinned down at me, his eyes crinkling in pleasant little lines of laughter.

"The Corporal was in good health when I saw him not more than a week since. He wrote this then, and asked me to bring it to you on my way home."

He took a letter from his saddlebag and held it out to me. The paper was warm from its closeness to the horse and the horseman, but to me it felt like the warmth of Robbie himself. I held it tightly in hands that shook. This small, warm, tangible fragment of Rob . . . involuntarily my eyes filled with tears. I missed him so terribly!

The man's voice was filled with concern as he dismounted quickly. "Ah, lass—you must not weep! I vow all was well with young Thomas when I saw him."

"Forgive me, please," I said unsteadily, "it is simply that it has been so long . . ." I tried to brush the tears away with the back of my hand. "Nigh three years now since I saw him, and this is the first word——" The tears began to pour again.

With the horse's reins looped over his arm, the man touched me gently on the shoulder and guided me to a stone wall beside the road. "Come, Mistress Sampson, sit here a moment." From a pocket he brought forth a handkerchief. "This is, I believe, reasonably clean."

I murmured my thanks, and wiped determinedly at my wet eyes and cheeks. "How did you know I was Deborah Sampson?" I asked shakily.

"The Corporal described you to me. He said I would likely find you hereabouts."

"He is a Corporal!" I marveled. "I did not know Robbie was a Corporal!" And then feminine curiosity compelled me to ask, "How did he describe me?"

The man put one foot on top of the wall and leaned on his bent knee. His dark eyes shone with amusement. "He told me to watch for a tall lass with a firm step, a piercing eye, and an angel's smile. It was not difficult to recognize you, save that I have seen little of the smile."

I half-laughed on a caught breath. "But more than enough of tears, I warrant." I sniffed the last dampness back. "There! All is well now. You are very kind to put up with such a deluge on a first meeting."

"So you do not remember," he said.

"Remember?"

"We have met before. Or perhaps we did not truly *meet*——"

And suddenly I recalled. "The news of Nat! 'Twas you brought that word to us!"

"Aye."

The thought of Nat threatened to bring the tears again, and quickly I forced it back. "You live near here?" I asked.

"North of here. A town called Sharon. I am an indifferent farmer, but I raise some cattle and horses that I deliver to the army. The way home often brings me through here, or so close as makes no difference."

"Will you see Robbie—Corporal Robert Thomas—again, do you think?"

"There is no way of knowing. If I do, what shall I tell him?"

I raised my eyes to look up at him directly. "I pray you will not mention the tears—that knowledge would not help him, I am sure."

There was an expression in his eyes I could not name. Kindness, understanding, sympathy, perhaps—all these, but something more. Approval? Admiration? It unsettled me.

"If I see the Corporal again, I shall tell him that when I last saw Mistress Sampson she was sitting, strong and straight, in the winter sunshine. I will tell him that her face glowed and filled me with its warmth. I will tell him that he is the most fortunate of men, and that I am in his debt to have been his messenger."

His eyes were steady on mine, and then his smile broke through. "Will that do?"

For a long second our eyes held. "Thank you," I said at last. "Thank you very much." I rose and started to move away when I realized I still held his handkerchief crumpled in my hand. I turned back to him. "Here. I fear it is thoroughly wet."

"In a good cause." He took the damp linen and thrust it into his pocket. "And there is no shame in weeping, lass—but sometimes laughing will help you more." He touched the brim of his dreadful old hat and swung himself up into the saddle, then turned and grinned down at me. "Remember that! Laughter can be of great benefit!"

I watched him start down the road. He did not look back. I ran home with my precious letter. It said little, but I treasured every word.

13 ☆ The Second Letter

Since I had stopped attending the First Congregational Church after Reverend Conant died, I had not transferred my allegiance to any other house of worship, and deep inside I felt the lack. As all young people were, I had been trained to sit through hour after hour of prayers and sermons every Sunday. In winter our hands would be stuffed into mittens or muffs or wrapped in shawls, our feet against small iron foot warmers filled with coals. In summer's heat we would surreptitiously blow gently, lower lip thrust out, hoping the slight air would dry the perspiration on our faces. It was not considered seemly to fan oneself in church meeting, no matter what the weather. We were permitted to bring "meeting seed," seeds of caraway or dill or the like, to chew on during the lengthy services, and even now the scent of those seeds instantly takes me back to the Middleborough church. With that association so much a part of me, I now felt it was time to renew my churchgoing habits, and I looked for a likely place.

In the spring of 1781, when I was twenty, the Third Baptist Church of Middleborough launched a great campaign to attract new members, and I was urged by several acquaintances to join. They were people I admired, firmly dedicated to their faith, and by autumn I saw no reason to hold back from their pressure, and I became a member. It was pleasant to resume my old habit of churchgoing, and I enjoyed the new friends I made. One of them, an earnest man named Ezra Henderson, spent much time in teaching me the ways of the Baptist church. But no matter how often I attended services, I could never find the warm, inspiring strength Reverend Conant had given me.

However, in the autumn of 1781, nothing else was as important as the magnificent news of a victorious battle in a Virginia city called Yorktown, which resulted in the surrender of the British General Cornwallis. Everyone agreed that at last the war was over, and a few weeks would see our men home again.

I could barely contain myself! To see Robbie again—to feel his arms around me and his lips hard against mine—to marry him and know the full extent of our love—to bear his children—it all seemed like heaven close at hand! But sometimes at night, when I turned restlessly and could not sleep, the small mouselike fears would begin to stir. It had been more than five years since I had seen Rob. I had changed, I was older, more serious, finding less to laugh at and less to content me. Then must not Rob have changed also? Would he still feel toward me as he had before? Would life still satisfy him if it held no more than a return to the fields, a return to me, a life with me and with the children I so much wanted? What had war done to him? For these long years he had lived a life in which I had no part. I could not imagine it, nor know what effect it might have had on him. I had talked to other young soldiers on their way home—sour, embittered men, warped not only in their physical beings, but in their minds as well. Rob had lived daily with all the things he loathed —pain, noise, killing. What would he be now? When a second letter came, delivered this time by a taciturn, raggedly-uniformed man with a blank stare, my hands shook so I could barely unfold the pages. "My own dearest Deborah," I read, and my heart filled with joy. Had the letter been written on a sheet of gold with a diamond quill, I could not have treasured it more. I read and reread it, until I knew it all by heart.

"My own dearest Deborah, As you know, I am not much of a hand at writing (and certainly not 'fancily') but with word of the victory at Yorktown I must share my pride in my country with someone, and it is always you I turn to. I have often felt a strong love for *America,* but now I feel it for *Americans* also. What a brave, staunch, diehard people we are! I have seen such courage displayed as I would not have believed, and—although I have hated almost every moment of soldiering—I have pledged myself to stay in the army until there is no further need. Such bravery must not be wasted, and though the war is considered by many to be over, there is still activity that comes from hard feelings. There are still small strongholds of British troops to be cleaned out, there is still plotting on their part against us, there are still brief (but bloody) skirmishes. Therefore I must stay until all reason for staying is done.

"In a way I am doing this for Nat, lest his death ever seem to have been useless. But it is for you, too, Deb, for you and for me. It has been years since I have seen you—and held you—years in which I have sometimes lost the shape of your face, but never doubted your love nor loyalty. There is a life ahead for us, and it must be in this country that I have helped to make our own. Your grandsires, who gave America life, would understand why I must do what I can to preserve that life. I hope you will understand, too.

"I am well, without a scratch to mark these years of warfare. (The British, thank the Lord, must not be as good marksmen as you!) When I come home we will have much to say to each other. God's will that day comes soon!

"My deepest love and respect to my parents. My heart to you.

Robbie."

And then, on a windblown March day, when the whitest of clouds scudded across a deep blue sky and the air smelled like spring, the word came that Robbie had been standing sentry duty while five companions slept. In the pale rays of moonlight his golden hair must have gleamed, a perfect target for the British shot that killed him.

We sat stunned and silent in the farmhouse kitchen. Mistress Thomas, frail and aged, clutched the crushed, soiled message from Robbie's captain, while the Deacon sat bent forward, his face buried in his hands.

Presently I left them and went silently out into the sunshine. Far down the fields I walked, past where the corn used to stand tall and straight, down to the spot where we had stood when Rob told me he was leaving. I knelt, and then I lay slowly down, trying to recall the warmth of a shoulder beneath my head, the quick rise and fall of a broad chest wherein the heart pounded. I dug my fingers deep into the long grass as into loved flesh, and curled my body in an agony of loss. And at last the tears came, stormily, wildly, and I wanted to scream out against a world that had robbed me of the one person I had felt to be mine. I crouched low, my arms wrapped close about myself, clutching my shoulders with my hands as though I could bring Robbie's embraces back to life, rocking to and fro in unbearable pain. I wanted to hurt as I was hurt, to kill as he had been killed. I cursed God in His heaven and felt no shame for my profanity.

But gradually the tears and sobbing slowed, and I lay back exhausted, my eyes stretched and dry, watching cloud castles form and change, and seeing nothing. Words seemed to drift through my head—remembered words and half-forgotten words. "It is something I *must* do . . . for Nat . . . for you . . . for myself. . . . I must stay until all reason for staying is done. . . . Such bravery must not be wasted. . . . I must do what I can to preserve that life. . . . When I come home, we will have much to say to each other. . . ."

He would not come home again, that bright-haired

man. He would never come home again. The end of love, the end of hope, the end of marriage and children —but not the end of fighting and death. The war still went on, and other women would mourn as I mourned now.

Perhaps that is when I knew what I had to do, although I did not recognize the thought on that sun-filled, dreadful day.

14 ☆ The Disgrace

A few weeks later I was back at the Leonards' house, doing my usual spinning and weaving. Life, I found, does go on. Jennie, that beautiful Negro girl of whom I was so fond, shared a bed with me, and as we lay at night waiting for sleep to take us, we talked. I told her of Robbie's death, and she wept for me, though I had no more tears.

"What will you do now, Deborah? You are not bound to the Thomases—what will you do?"

"I don't know, Jennie. Rob hated the thought of going to war—now I hate the thought of staying here without him. I wish I could be someplace else, doing something that *mattered!* I can't just *spin* my life away—I want to use all my mind, all my energies on something important. Something for *Robbie!*" Suddenly I sat up straight in bed. "Jennie, I want to join the army!"

"You!" Her voice was unbelieving. "What are you talking about? You are just funning, aren't you, Deborah?"

"No! No, Jennie, I'm not funning!" I turned to her

quickly, excited, the words tripping over themselves. "Jennie, do you think I could pass for a man? In men's clothes, with my hair tied back—I am tall, Jennie, taller than a lot of men! And I can do most anything a man can do. I can shoot, and ride, and I am strong! Jennie, do you think I could pass as a man?"

"You don't exactly have a man's shape, Deborah—you're not exactly *flat!*"

"I could tie a binder round myself, a tight one, with a vest over that, and a shirt, and a jacket——"

"Deborah, I think you're plumb crazy! How do you think you could live with a whole army of men and not have them know you for a woman?"

"I don't know, but I think I am going to try."

"Deborah, how would you even take a *bath?*"

And suddenly I laughed. I was filled with a glorious excitement, with a purpose, with a reason for living. If Robbie could not see the war out, then I would do it for him! Never mind how—that could come later. Now I had a plan, a design. I could barely wait to get on with it.

"Maybe I'll never bathe, Jennie. Right now that does not seem to matter. But tomorrow you are going to help me find some clothes, and we're going to queue my hair back, and we're going to flatten down my bosom, and I'm going to enlist in the army, Jennie! Some way I am going to do it!"

Jennie sighed deeply. "Deborah Sampson, you are a crazy, stubborn woman!" Then she giggled. "But I'll help!"

That night I slept very little.

Jennie found me the suit of clothes. It belonged to the Leonards' son, who had given it up for a uniform. I stand five feet seven and a half inches tall, and most men are about five feet four inches. Master Leonard's breeches rode low on my hips, and my wrists showed below the coat sleeves. But with a binder tight around my breasts, my hair tied back in a masculine queue, my legs looking long and slim (and shameless!) in breeches, I made a remarkably credible male. Jennie clasped her hands in laughing delight.

"I vow you are better looking than a lot of honest-to-God men I've seen! Just keep your voice down, take big steps, and don't scream if you see a snake!"

"I have never screamed when I saw a snake," I answered her with dignity, and then hugged her tight. "Oh, Jennie! Do you really think I can do it?"

"I'm not making any promises on as flighty an idea as this, but if *any* woman could do it—then I reckon you're the woman!"

I finished my work at the Leonards' in the next few days, trying on my new clothes from time to time in an effort to become accustomed to them. They made me feel a very different person, filled with dedication and a sense of excitement. In such clothes I could dare to get away from the painfully familiar places and see something of this country for which my man had died. If Robbie and I could not be joined through marriage, then let us be joined through a common experience.

What he had not been able to finish, I would finish for him.

I told no one but Jennie of my intentions. If I was promptly discovered and sent back in disgrace I wanted no one laughing at me. I was beholden to no one, and no one was responsible for me. It should not matter where I went nor what I did. I told the Thomases I planned to go farther north and find more spinning and weaving work, a lie which they accepted quietly, wishing me well.

And so, on a late April afternoon I strode away with my new long steps, heading for the enlistment office in the home of one Master Israel Wood.

On opening the door, I panicked. The small room was crowded with young men, jostling around in a ragged line by a high desk, behind which stood a dusty little man, spectacles sliding down his nose, busily writing. It seemed that every eye in the room turned to look at me, and I was sure they saw through my useless disguise and knew me for what I was. I started to back out the door, but my arm was caught by one of the men.

"What's the matter, laddie, changed your mind already?"

"As a matter of truth—yes," I said, trying to escape.

"Now we can't have that! A healthy boy like you—your army needs you! Sign up, young man, don't be a coward!" And he pushed me in front of him in the line.

I wanted nothing so much as to get out of there, but short of a physical struggle with the man behind me (and probably those in front of me, too) I could see no way to accomplish it, so there I stood, my heart beating violently from my own foolishness. Another moment or two, and I was in front of the high desk.

"Name?" inquired the dusty little man, apparently Master Wood. He barely looked at me, just held his quill poised over a paper.

"Timothy Thayer," I heard myself say, and could not imagine where the name had come from.

"Age?" he asked, and I suddenly thought of my unbearded face and subtracted several years from my age.

"Ah—seventeen," I murmured.

There were one or two more questions which I somehow answered, and then he rattled off something about I was now a member of the Continental Army to serve for a term of three years for the good of my country and to appear the following morning for the regimental roll call and here was my forty pounds. With that he shoved money into my hand, called, "Next recruit," and I was pushed toward the door.

It was done, and I could not believe it!

Outside was a group of men who had signed on ahead of me, all in the best of spirits.

"A little something to wet our whistles," one of them said, and there was an immediate chorus of agreement. Two of them laid friendly arms across my shoulders, and then we were all marching down the road that led to Sproat's Tavern.

I could see no way of removing myself without causing a disturbance, and I assured myself that I would drink one glass of wine or cider and then depart. Ah me! If I only had!

Never had I met such amiable men! I was still terrified of being discovered, and I said little, but within a few minutes it seemed we had known each other all our lives. Each one must buy a round of drinks for his fellows, and there was no mention of the cider or wine I had envisioned. They had bounty money in their purses, time on their hands, and a thirst in their gullets that would be assuaged by nothing less than the strongest liquors they could order. Mild drink was not strange to me, but the "firewater" that kept arriving at our long table created havoc with my brain.

I remember wanting to appear as masculine as possible, even while I became fuddled with drink. I could hear a voice I dimly recognized as mine roaring out that I was "Timothy Thayer, I was strong, I was free," and later there was a great thumping on the table by poor, misguided Master Thayer and orders for drinks all round. Later still—what a spectacle I must have made!—there were oceans of tears for a golden-haired friend who would come home no more. Oh, Deborah! How could you have behaved so!

My next recollection is of being distressingly ill in the dooryard of the tavern, supported on either side by tight-lipped acquaintances from the Baptist church, who at last led me back to the Thomas household. My feet dragged, my head was sunk low, and shame filled me so I could not speak. Mrs. Thomas silently helped me to bed, and through unpleasantly shifting clouds of darkness and light I slept.

Sometime the next morning I opened eyes that felt like hot coals, raised my hand to a head that resembled an earthquake in progress, and became aware that my mouth must have been stuffed with unwashed sheep's wool. Mistress Thomas was standing by the bed, holding a wet cloth and a tankard.

Laying the cloth, cool and welcome, across my forehead, she raised me up slightly and held the tankard to my lips.

"Drink this," she said. "Drink it down quickly." I thought I would retch, but I managed to swallow the contents. "There are people waiting to see you," she added.

"People?"

"Ezra Henderson and a friend from the Baptist church—they brought you home last night—and some officials from Master Wood's enlistment office. Shall I tell them you will see them, Deborah?"

I felt far too mortified and ill to see anyone, but penance had to be done.

"Yes. I will dress and see them now."

It was a degrading meeting. The officials demanded the return of the bounty money, and I had to make up what I had spent at Sproat's Tavern—an awesome amount!—from my small savings. They then threatened me with a dreadful fate if I ever visited the recruiting office again, and took themselves off. My two brethen from the Baptist church insisted that I kneel and pray with them so that I would be cleansed of my sins, but it was physically impossible. Begging their forgiveness I excused myself, returning to my room. There I fell on the bed, shamed, disgraced, and filled with self-loathing. How could my great resolve, my crusade, my gesture of love for Robbie and faith in my country, have descended to this deplorable situation?

I lay for some hours, staring at the familiar ceiling, and at last I settled on three facts. The first, that I should never again imbibe strong liquor in any quantity; the second, that I had been able to pass myself off as a young man until I was undone by drink; and the third, that I could no longer stay with the Thomases, inflicting my shame upon them.

My resolution to continue Robbie's fight where he had been forced to lay it down was stronger than ever, for now I also needed to restore my personal pride. If I could do it once, I could do it again, but this time with forethought, dignity, and planning.

And so, for the second time, I enlisted in the Continental Army.

15 ☆ Private Robert Shurtlieff

I look at the words I have just written, and they make it sound as though it had been a simple procedure. It was not. It took several weeks. From woolen cloth that belonged to me, which I had spun and woven for myself, I stitched man's clothing (since young Leonard's garments had long since been returned to his room). From the Thomases' house I took nothing but the small amount of money that was mine. And thus I left, unseen, in the pre-dawn of a May morning, with no adieux and no explanations.

Obviously I would have to go farther afield than Israel Wood's recruiting office, but I did not know where. It took me a deal of walking. A long and circuitous route, through many towns, brought me at last to Bellingham, where I learned that the neighboring village of Uxbridge needed recruits to fill its quota.

And there, on May 20, 1782, young "Robert Shurtlieff" enlisted in the Continental Army for a term of three years.

The first part of my new name was for Robbie, of course. The last was because it was a common name in that part of Massachusetts, spelled in several different ways, and might, I felt, sound legitimate while being somewhat difficult to trace. It was never questioned, and I sheltered behind that name for a long time. It is still somehow a part of me.

I was told to report to Worcester three days hence, where I would be "mustered in." This I did, and was given a bounty of sixty pounds by one Noah Taft, Chairman of Class Number Two. "Robert Shurtlieff" signed the receipt, "his" hand a little shaky when forced to the unfamiliar name. And so I became a Private in the Fourth Massachusetts Regiment, commanded by Colonel William Shepard, and assigned to a light infantry company under Captain George Webb. It was a part of General John Paterson's brigade.

Almost immediately we were formed up for the march to West Point and the beginning of a strange life for Robert Shurtlieff. As for that tall, restless, heartbroken female, Deborah Sampson, she no longer existed.

We must have looked a haphazard lot as we marched along! A very young drummer boy had been assigned to us, and he tried bravely to beat out a rhythm that we would follow, but for the first day or so it was rare to find four men abreast who were in step. As we crossed the state of Connecticut and the days went by, our appearance improved, and certainly our knowledge of each other did. We were permitted to talk together (if we had the breath to do so), and it was interesting to hear something of the men with whom I now belonged. As for me, I was Robert Shurtlieff, I came from a village near Plymouth, I was seventeen. I was one of a large family, but had left home for the army. Only part of it was true, but since my present life was in every way a lie, I made it as convincing a lie as possible.

Ten days is a long time to march, but each day gave me more confidence in my new character and I began to regard the whole adventure as good sport. It had seemed to me that bathing, physical evacuation, and dressing or undressing would be my greatest hazards, but now I felt I had fretted needlessly. There was no thought of bathing on that march, and we slept in our clothes. As for physical needs, there were wooded areas, vine-covered stone walls, or an occasional farmhouse privy, and I made use of them.

I appeared to be as strong as most of my male companions, who dropped to the ground as exhausted as I whenever a halt was called. We slept on the ground, which was strange to me, but I believe I could have slept on the sharp end of iron nails had I been told to.

One morning we woke to a steady rainfall, cold as even May rain can be. All that day we marched, splashing through puddles, soaked to our skins, chilled to the bone, covered with mud. Our officers liking it no more than ourselves, we were ordered to stop at a roadside tavern during the early evening.

I was lightheaded from fatigue and hunger, having eaten nothing since a scant and early (and wet) breakfast, and when I stood before the roaring fire in the tavern I was astonished to find that quite suddenly the voices around me were fading into a blurred distance. The next I knew I was stretched on the floor by the fire, my head in the comfortable lap of a woman who was crooning over me.

"Poor boy! He's exhausted! And drenched through! If some of you men will help me get him up the stairs and undressed, he can sleep in my husband's bed for a bit. My husband has been snoring these two hours past and will not be disturbed."

Not even Gabriel's trumpet could have roused me faster! I sat up abruptly, my head swimming.

"Oh no, ma'am! You are most kind, but no! I shall be all right in a moment or two—the fire is so pleasantly warm. See? My clothes are drying already!"

My clothes were indeed sending off gentle clouds of steam, but it seemed unlikely that they would be dry for some time to come. I mustered up a smile, and tried to look both masculine and well recovered.

"Some food is all I need, and surely we are in the right place for that! No need to fret about us, ma'am. We are used to this sort of minor discomfort."

One of the recruits muttered that *he* was not used to it, but he was told by another that he had best become so because, from all *he* had heard, this was a good sample of army life. In any case, the kindly matron left me to the fire and some hot food and retired to her husband's bed. Far better she than I!

Except for that brief weakness I believe I withstood the march as well as any of the men. In the afternoon of the tenth day we came to the banks of the Hudson River, crossed it by ferry, and had arrived at the famed Military Fortress of West Point.

16 ☆ A Soldier's Life

There are many things that have happened to me over the years which I may have forgotten, but never—*never!*—will I forget that first day at the Fortress. Poor deluded Deborah! Her one wish was to burst into tears and run home to Mrs. Thomas!

After those ten days of marching, living as a man with other men, I was filled with confidence that I could continue easily, and without fear of discovery, on this strange path I had set myself. As we lined up and were issued uniforms and equipment, I admired all that I was given and handled it with pride. As a member of the First Brigade I received a blue coat lined with white, a white waistcoat, breeches and stockings, black garters, half boots, a black velvet stock and a most beautiful cap. It bore a variegated cockade on one side, and a plume tipped with red on the other. Around the crown was a white sash, or ribbon. My equipment consisted of a knapsack, a cartridge box and cartridges, a French musket with its ugly bayonet, a blanket, and a haversack. Canteens we had to purchase for ourselves. (Before many weeks I had added a hatchet and jackknife, though often in the months to come I would be tempted to discard the whole lot and travel unencumbered.)

With my arms loaded, I was herded innocently into a large room where half a hundred men were in various stages of undress. My throat choked, I am sure my face was scarlet, and my eyes tried desperately to find some focus other than the men around me. Where was my brave unconcern now? Had I truly thought the army would provide snug and private chambers, or had I not thought at all? Only one thing helped me keep some fraction of control. Undergarments, of course, were not removed, since they are changed only in spring and fall, and this was June. Except for one or two "dandies" in the room who chose to wash before donning their fine new garments–thereby leaving themselves open to jibes from the other men–none of them stripped to their skins. Even so, I felt drowned in masculinity, and I am sure that if anyone had bothered to watch they would have been astounded at the speed with which I slipped out of each piece of my civilian's clothing, replacing it immediately with its counterpart in the uniform. With garters unfastened, stockings sliding around my legs, black velvet stock flying open, I fled from the room and sagged on a bench outside. There I tried to regain my regular breathing, and gradually put myself together. Once dressed I began to feel a reassuring anonymity, and a sudden interest in my uniform. I quite fancied myself in it!

As the other men came out we were shown where we would sleep–oh, those long rows of bunks, all to be filled with men except for one, occupied by a demented Deborah Sampson!—and were told to rid ourselves of our old clothing and excess equipment. Then, lined up in neat formation, we were marched to another building. This, we were told by a burly sergeant, was the regimental outhouse, and he threw open the door with pride, releasing an appalling stench.

Inside were long raised planks into which had been drilled a series of round holes. Some of the men took immediate and joyous advantage of the opportunity to relieve themselves, while my teeth gritted in agony and my eyes must have rolled like those of a frenzied horse. The sergeant warned that there was a scarcity of candles, and advised us all to make use of the outhouse in the daylight. Solemnly I vowed that if I had to walk all day with my legs crossed I would somehow wait till the darkest hours of night.

From there we were directed to an adjoining room where a dozen or so tall barrels lined one wall. If anyone wanted to bathe, explained our guide in a manner that indicated he had little respect for those who might, the barrels could be filled with water. Other than that there was the river, close at hand, and available for swimming. I found some small comfort in the fact that while swimming seemed to appeal to the men for the sport of it, bathing had little importance in their lives. I remembered with awful clarity Jennie's shocked question, "Deborah, how would you take a *bath?*" It looked as if I would not.

At last we were fed, meagerly and unappetizingly,

and sent off to the barracks. Exhausted, emotionally and physically, I removed my outer garments in the blessedly dim light from two small candles placed at either end of the room, and safe in my concealing undergarments, fell onto the hard bed. Around me arose an evening concert of ribald remarks, deep laughter, nose-blowing, hawking and spitting, grunts, and—eventually—snores. Lying straight and stiff and wide-eyed in the dark I tried to gather my willpower together. I had determined to join the army, I had come this far, and—heaven help me!—I could not give up now. But I could see I was going to have to be prepared for things I had not considered.

My first stern lecture to myself, lying there in the heavily breathing dark, was to lose my shock at the sight of the male body. I told myself firmly that God had created us all, men and women alike, and His handiwork should not be a cause for shame nor embarrassment. Calm acceptance of *many* things would have to be my watchword.

My next thought was that the normally simple matter of emptying myself was going to require greater planning. The more I thought on this, the more I realized that there was an immediate need. Turn and twist as I might, there could be no further delay. As quietly as I could I slid out of my bunk and tiptoed silently across the creaking floor, a timorous ghost in my white garments. I had nearly reached the outside door when there came a grunt and a movement from one of the beds.

"Is aught wrong, boy?" a sleepy voice inquired.

I stopped dead. "N-n-no, sir. I just need—I mean—I have to—"

"Well, don't use the floor. Go outside. Place smells like a pigpen already."

"Yes, sir."

And out I went. Moonlight bathed everything in a clear white glow, and I felt as if I were watched by a hundred invisible eyes. Skulking in what shadow I could find, moving as quickly as clenched muscles would allow, I reached the dim bulk of the outhouse. I pushed open the door on total blackness. Suppose there were someone there—suppose, in that darkness, we touched! Lowering my voice to its deepest pitch I said softly, "Anyone in here?" There was no sound. By touch (and smell!) I found the nearest of the holes and sat me down.

That was a strange moment! The physical relief of emptying myself, the strain of the long day, the fears and worries and shocks, all combined and I found myself weeping helplessly. How could I go on with this imposture? It seemed impossible. I felt more alone than ever in my life, and sure that I could never continue what now seemed the foolhardiest of plans. If something as commonplace as the need for evacuation could leave me sitting straight and in tears in the middle of the night . . . Suddenly there was a faint brush of memory. What was it? Something to do with sitting straight . . . and tears . . . A voice! "Ah, lass—you must not weep!" Who had said that? When? That man! That tall, dark man whose name I did not know—the one who had brought the first letter from

Robbie—whose eyes had held warm admiration when he looked at me—what had he said? "Sometimes laughing will help you more." Surprisingly I giggled. Oh, my dear man! My dear, vigorous, smiling, nameless man! If you could see me now! My laughter grew uncontrollable as I thought, where is that face, "glowing in the winter sunlight?" Where is that young woman, "sitting straight and strong?" Where but here, here in a pitch-black outhouse, formally dressed in masculine undergarments! It was so ridiculous! I laughed until I was weak, and with the laughter came a new resolve. "Each day as it comes," I thought. "I have contrived to get through the first, I shall do my best to manage each as it comes to pass. It will not be easy, but—with laughter—perhaps a little easier."

Bless that man! The laughter had helped. It seemed to bring this strange life back to some sort of normalcy. The time in the outhouse helped also. I returned to my bed, pulled my blanket over me, and fell into a deep slumber. I may very well have snored as loudly as the rest.

It was still dark at four o'clock the next morning when we were awakened by a demanding drumbeat. Sure that the British had surrounded the Fortress and that I would be thrown into immediate battle, I leapt into my uniform, snatched up my musket, and was out the door while most of the men were still rubbing their sleep-laden eyes and groaning their way out of bed.

The morning was quiet and peaceful, and the only signs of invasion were a few sleepy soldiers making their way to the outhouse. Off to the left I noted a wooded area of small, closely-set trees. Casting a quick eye around and finding myself unobserved, I made my way some few lengths into the wood, found a small and concealing thicket, and dropped my breeches. It took no more than a moment or two, and from then on those cherished woods became my personal privy. By exerting self-control, taking advantage of any likely moment, and making midnight trips to the deserted outhouse to empty my bowels (which earned me the nickname of "Baby Bladder" when I made my nightly exits from the barracks), I somehow managed.

The four o'clock reveille came every morning. We gathered on the regimental parade ground for military drill, and I found myself enjoying the unison and precision of the exercise. I acquired dexterity in handling my musket, though the thought of using that bayonet on a living being froze my blood, and I mastered the Manual of Arms quickly, gaining a few words of grudging praise from Sergeant Calvin Munn.

The days were fully occupied in military training, with little free time. Some of the men used these rare hours to shuck off their clothes and swim in the river, a sport I envied them, though I have never been at home in the water. It took only a few days to lose any feeling of shock at seeing my companions undressed. They were so completely at ease, it seemed only natural to react in the same way. The nearest I came to washing myself was an occasional cold sponge around my exposed areas. It was not thorough, but it was as much as most of the men did, and more than some. We were without question a highly-scented lot, but that, too, I learned to take with "calm acceptance."

For the most part I came to consider myself not as "woman" nor as "female" but as "soldier." I have always addressed myself in my thoughts, but now it was, "Robert, you must do thus and so," or "See here, Private Shurtlieff, that was a very clumsy bayonet maneuver!" Only once in those first weeks can I recall speaking to myself as "Deborah," and that was when I reached my period. "Oh, Deborah, *now* what do you do!" I groaned. Fortunately I was always regular, so it was predictable, and my flow was slight. A surreptitious packing and a light bandage applied in that midnight outhouse, and changed once or twice in the dusky privacy of the woods, with the evidence buried, and I managed. Young women nowadays may well be horrified at such casual methods. I can only say to them that what a person *must* do, he (or she!) does.

17 ☆ The First Encounter

I soon discovered that belonging to the Light Infantry was considered an honor. The men chosen for it were young, agile, and good shots, and I was told that when in the field the Light Infantry was placed nearest the enemy. They must, consequently, be always alert and watchful. After some weeks of training, when I was confident I knew all a soldier should know, I was given my first taste of this "honor."

In the minds of most people the war was actually over. With the surrender of Burgoyne and Cornwallis the British army was restrained to an area in and around New York City. In theory there was a truce between the two armies, but in fact feelings ran so high on both sides that there were often clashes between scouting or foraging parties. Early in June I was included in a detachment that was sent southward to spy on British movements.

We crossed the river at Stony Point and marched over rough trails to Tarrytown, which was considered a neutral area between the American and English lines. There we split into several small groups to cover a wider territory, with orders to note enemy troop positions.

With another soldier—a cocky bantam rooster of a man named Nathan—I approached a farmhouse, taking advantage of every bit of concealment. From a wooded patch across the road I lifted my head carefully and was dumbfounded to find I had an uncomfortably close view of The Enemy. In the dooryard of the farmhouse six or eight Redcoats were reclining peacefully on the ground, smoking their clay pipes and talking quietly. One was chewing on a chicken leg, and my stomach growled in envy.

I nudged Nate and pointed. With a delighted expression on his ruddy face he deliberately raised his musket and took aim. Without thinking I grasped the barrel of his gun and pushed the muzzle against the ground.

"Don't be a fool, Nate," I whispered. "You could only get one, and the rest of them would get us!"

"But I have to get me an Englishman," he muttered back. "I've had nary a chance to get me an Englishman!"

"You will find a better chance than this," I told him, and reluctantly he followed me away from there, unseen by the relaxed enemy.

But as we moved undiscovered away from Tarrytown and neared a place called, strangely, Sing Sing, Nate's desire became too great for him. We crept along two hundred yards or so from small clusters of British dragoons, and watched them polishing muskets and boots, filling paper cartridges, taking their ease in the warm June sun. With no warning Nathan stood erect behind me, lifted his musket, and fired.

"I got me an Englishman!" he shouted just before he fell with a single scream at my feet from gunfire promptly returned. Stupefied, I looked down at him. Nate's face no longer existed. Quite suddenly I vomited on the ground. An instant later I was in the middle of a small but deadly battle, with only one thought in my mind, to stay alive.

What is a battle like? It is noise and smoke and confusion. It is shouting and shooting, it is fear and anger, it is killing someone before he kills you first, it is instinctively doing what you have been taught to do. All I had learned about self-preservation and annihilation of the enemy fused into one white shaft of fury. As fast as I could tear open a paper cartridge with my teeth, pour the explosive powder into the musket, and ram home the lead ball and the two buckshot, I fired. My mind noted the two Redcoats that I felled, but I felt no emotion about them.

From heaven knows where, Loyalist enforcements joined the British, and the enemy fire became so thick that we retreated to a heavily wooded area that gave us more protection. It seemed as though the firing went on for days, but it could not have been more than an hour or so before we were joined by—of all people!—Colonel Ebenezer Sproat, late of Sproat's Tavern! Behind him came a goodly number of his Second Massachusetts Regiment, and in short order the Americans were in control.

It was not until then that I realized I had caught a British ball in my right shoulder. I was terrified! Not by the wound itself, nor by the pain, but at the thought of a doctor's examination. Surely work on my shoulder would disclose my breast, and I had not come this far to be discovered and sent off in disgrace. When I was questioned about the blood I said it had come from a wounded comrade, and the matter was not pursued.

Late that night, by the light of a campfire and with the aid of my jackknife, I tried to remove the ball. Since it was in my right shoulder I had to use my left hand, with which I have never been skillful, and the clumsy probing, done in flickering firelight, achieved nothing but exquisite pain. Unable to pry the bullet out, alone and frightened, I sat hunched by the small fire, weeping desolately, yearning for Mrs. Thomas's deft hands, for Jennie's practical help—for *someone!*

At last, when the physical pain had eased, I wet my handkerchief with water from my canteen, washed my tear-streaked face and then the wound, wadded the handkerchief over the open sore, and held it in place with the tight binder that covered my bosom. I used more of the water to rinse the blood from my coat, and then there was nothing left that I could do.

For a few days my arm was sore indeed, and any movement close to agony. But the wound was a clean one, I was blessed with good health, and by the time a week had passed my shoulder gave me little trouble. It was the nightmare vision of Nate, lying at my feet with bloody pulp where his face had been, that I could not shut out of my mind.

18 ☆ The Hospital

I am not sure how I had envisioned life in the Continental Army—with a certain number of romantic notions, I suppose, and also with the feeling that I would be making some great gesture to Robbie, that I would be completing a task he had set for himself, which he had not been allowed to finish. It had seemed a consuming thing, almost a holy thing, that I would be doing for the man I had loved so much. Perhaps men sometimes have similar reasons for enlisting. I think some of them do.

In reality there was little to keep us occupied. We drilled, we marched, we learned to defend ourselves and demolish our opponents, we filled cartridges, we cleaned our quarters—usually far better than we cleaned ourselves. We ate scant, unappetizing food, we slept from boredom, rather than from fatigue. It no longer seemed strange to be constantly surrounded by men. Without thinking, I spoke in a deeper voice than was normal, I walked with a longer, easier stride, I wore my uniform naturally. I was as tall as many of the men, and taller than some, and the years of physical work I had enjoyed on the Thomas farm had given me sufficient strength for anything I was expected to do.

If I was lonely, that could not be helped. I spent leisure time a little apart from the others, and was teased for being a "schoolboy at his books" because I liked to read. The men were friendly enough, and on occasion they sought my "schoolboy" abilities by asking me to write letters home for them. It was surprising how many of my comrades could neither read nor write. I was also useful as a replacement for the regimental barber when the men's queues needed greasing, rebraiding, and—for the dandies among us—powdering.

All in all, army life at West Point was disappointing in its lack of military activity, but I was determined to remain in uniform until the war was officially declared over. That was what Robbie had intended, and that was what I could do for him. When volunteers were requested to flush out armed Tories from East Chester, I quickly added my name to the list.

By now my shoulder rarely bothered me, and even the burden of full equipment was not uncomfortable. With about thirty others I left West Point late in June of 1782. After an uneventful march of a few days we made camp one night at a place called Vonhoite, where, after the usual scant meal, I fell asleep. I was dreaming hungrily of hot rabbit stew when the guard sounded the alarm. In quick whispers we were alerted to the approach of a small group of armed and mounted British troops. A moment later there was a burst of gunfire, and the two sides were joined. In the faint starlight it was impossible to see clearly what was happening. I grasped the arm of a well-filled red coat, only to see the other arm raised in the air, the hand gripping a sword. Obeying those weeks of training I threw my weight against the sword arm, diverting a blow which would certainly have put an end to Robert Shurtlieff. Instead, I felt a sharp crack against my head before the point of my bayonet found its mark, and the man fell at my feet. As I stepped back I felt a tremendous thud close to my groin which knocked me to the ground. Dizzy and breathless, I pulled myself to my knees, watching for another move from the enemy, but they had taken themselves off and the brief battle was over. I collapsed slowly to the ground again, weakened, stunned, in pain, and in tears.

Several Tories had been killed, but only one Continental. There were, however, a number who were wounded, of which I was one. Covered with blood from the gash on my head and the wound in my thigh, I must have made an awesome picture to the first of my comrades who approached me. He started to help me to my feet.

"Come," he said, "I'll get you to a hospital, Robbie."

Hospital! Doctors who would look for that musket ball would find something more unexpected! Anything rather than that, I thought desperately. Perhaps, if I were left alone–

"No, leave me here! The wound is mortal–take yourself off! You must not risk yourself for me!" I tried to sound firm and commanding, but my voice shook.

"The French have a hospital at Crompond. It is not more than six miles off. You will be taken care of there."

"No, please no! Just leave me!"

But they would not listen. I was lifted by my comrades, placed before one of them on a horse, and galloped off to the hospital. Lying across the horse's back, being unmercifully jounced, blood dripping from my head and my leg, my shoulder awakened into sudden pain, I prayed sincerely that I would die before we reached the hospital. I lay there, head hanging, and saw the pistol that was holstered to the saddle. Somehow I got my hand on it. Perhaps I was delirious, but my only thought was: I must not be discovered as a female! I had almost raised the pistol to my head with every serious intention of using it, when that cursed fellow saw what I was doing.

"You bloody stupid lout," he roared, and snatched the gun away from me. That was my last chance. I was carried into the hospital and deposited unceremoniously on a table where I lay exhausted, weak from loss of blood, filled with pain, and unable to move.

Almost immediately a French doctor came breezily into the room, carrying two bottles of wine. Opening them both, he passed them around to me and to the other wounded men who had been brought in from the same skirmish, and then proceeded to examine us. I had time to have several strong pulls from the bottle before he was at my side, and they helped to clear my head so I could think.

"So very early in the morning," he said cheerily. "How do you lose so much blood so early in the morning? First we will wash so we can see what damage has been done."

He carefully cleaned my face and head, and then bound up the sword wound on my scalp.

"Alors! That is better, no?"

"Much better. Yes," I replied, the strength of the wine flowing through me.

"We give you clean clothes now, and then you will sleep. A few days' rest and you will feel like a new man."

"Thank you," I said, and sat up on the table. The movement drove a great poker of pain through my groin, but determinedly I slid off the table to my feet and accepted the fresh white garment I was given. I started to limp from the room to change when I was stopped by that all too observant Frenchman.

"What is this? You cannot walk—and your boot! It is filled with blood! Sit down!"

"No, really, doctor, there is nothing wrong with me." I took two more lurching steps toward the door before he grasped my shoulder, turned me around, and sat me in a chair.

"Your boot say you lie," he said, and before I could stop him he had pulled off my boots and stockings, but, happily, not my breeches. By a miracle the wound in my thigh must have ceased to bleed, so that when he had washed my lower leg there was no trace of a wound.

"You see?" I said cockily. "There is nothing. Allow me to change my clothes, and if I find any other injury I shall tell you."

He looked unconvinced, but at last moved to the far side of the room and busied himself with another man, his back toward me. I had spied what I needed, and now I quickly picked up a silver probe, some lint and bandages, and the pot of salve the doctor had used on my head. Holding them under the clean clothing, I started to leave the room, but I paused just long enough to take a last swig of wine. I was going to need all the courage I could get!

Undressed and alone, I found that the ball had penetrated some two inches into the very top of my thigh. The first probing was so agonizing I feared I would faint, but it had to be done. Strangely enough, I did not cry. On the third attempt I removed the ball, covered the ugly hole with salve, pressed the lint tightly over it, and held it in place with the bandage. With sweat dripping from my forehead and my hands shaking, I put the loose wrapper on over my concealing undergarments, and went back to the larger room.

"Eh bien," that suspicious Frenchman said. "Give me those filthy clothes. They will be washed for you. Now you will sleep."

"Yes," I agreed. "That is all I need." And with no further conversation I lay down on a straw-filled mattress that felt like a velvet couch and drifted away from the world.

That happy state had existed for not more than an

hour when he returned, holding my breeches in his hand. They were dripping water, and he thrust his fingers into a rent in one leg.

"This hole," he said accusingly. "What makes this hole? A musket ball, no?"

"Oh no! It was a . . . ah . . . a nail in the saddle. When my friends brought me here. Just a nail, sir. Nothing else."

"Hah!" was all he said, but I was sure he did not believe me.

"If I may sleep now . . . I have had little rest the last few nights. That is all I need."

And then he said "Hmm," but he left, taking the offending breeches, and I fell back into a deep slumber.

My head mended quickly, and as I improved *Monsieur le Docteur* became less suspicious of me, but I was still eager to get away from his gimlet eyes, and before the wound in my thigh was half healed I rejoined my company. It took all my strength to walk the necessary miles, but anything was better than waiting for that bright-eyed Frenchman to discover the sex of his patient!

19 ☆ A Boastful Private Shurtlieff

In many ways life in the army reminded me of my life with the Thomas boys. There was the same lustiness, the same joking, the same rivalry in physical prowess. Some of the language used by the men with whom I lived was far saltier than anything the Thomases had ever uttered, and I believe those men would have died of shame had they known female ears were listening. There was virtually nothing about men that I did not learn during those months. I saw them on their best behavior and on their worst. I saw them sick and well, brave and cowardly, drunk and sober, dressed and naked. I was accepted as one of them, and called "Rob" or "Robbie" by those my own age. Those who were older sometimes called me "laddie" and teased me about my "smock face." It was only by devious questioning that I found they meant the smooth, unwhiskered complexion of a little boy, young enough to wear a smock rather than breeches.

They often talked of the female conquests they had made, frequently boasting, I am sure. To listen to some of them, one would think there was not an untouched young woman remaining in all the thirteen colonies, and this I *knew* was untrue. There was—at the very least—one.

I remember an occasion when that "one" was uncovered, and almost *dis*covered. I can laugh now, but I nigh swooned then! An undeniable call of nature had taken me into the woods to my "private privy." It was late on a gray spring afternoon, and the ground was muddied from several days of rain. I found a fallen log I had used many times before, untied the strings that held my breeches in place, folded back the flaps, and let them drop. Comfortably seated on my log I was struck with panic to hear footsteps and deep voices, far too close to allow time for covering my nether regions with my drooping breeches. Terrified, I did the only thing I could think of to do—rolled backwards off the log, dropped behind it, and made myself as small as possible. Tense and still, I huddled there, my clothes soaking up the puddled rainwater and my own body wastes. The steps and voices passed me, and after a moment—during which I was sure the beating of my heart would be heard—I dared to rise to my knees and pull up my drawers and breeches. Cautiously I stood, but there was no one in sight. A look at my clothing showed it mud-stained, soaked, and reeking with filth, but there was naught to do save summon every ounce of courage and walk back to the barracks. As I came out of the woods a small group of my companions stood talking together, and one of them looked up as I passed.

"Great thundering heavens, Rob—what have you been doing? Where have you been?"

"Looks to me as if he's been rolling in the pigsty," said another.

"Or rolling a lusty wench in a mud puddle!"

"Was that it, Rob? I've seen you head for those woods before! Are you hiding some sweet lassie there?"

"Two or three of them," I said bravely, trying to pass. "I had better wash these breeks—"

The men laughed. "If you're keeping females in the woods," one said, " 'tis for nothing more than to play Ring Around a Rosie, I'll be bound! You're too young for more than that."

"Do they want other games, Rob? Tell us! We'll show them men's games!"

I could not resist a last remark. "If you do, beware," I said, smiling. "Men's games are but child's play compared to women's!"

In the barracks I exchanged my sodden, reeking breeches for the mended ones that had roused the French doctor's suspicion, and carried the others down to the river where I washed them. I was still shaken. Had those soldiers who entered the wood not made their presence so readily known, poor Robert Shurtlieff would have been caught in the most compromising of positions, for which there could have been only one explanation—the right one. It made me realize afresh how constantly I had to be on my guard.

It may have been the men's opinion of me as a callow and thoroughly innocent youth that led me into a dangerously boastful conversation not long after that.

There was never enough food, although West Point was said to be better supplied than many of the other bases, and one summer evening I wandered through the depleted countryside looking for something to buy or to steal to augment the meals. I had been joined by a tall, burly, weathered soldier named Thomas Potter. He was perhaps ten years older than I, and rough-spoken, but a good-hearted man and a brave soldier. In a soft twilight we stopped and built a small campfire. Thomas let himself down on the ground beside me.

"Where the bloomin' blazes do you think we are, laddie?" he asked.

"The Fortress is just over there," I pointed. "Not more than ten miles."

"One place looks just like another here. Just as full of trees and just as empty of food."

"Perhaps not quite as empty." I reached into one of my big pockets and carefully brought out four large eggs.

"Bowl me over! Where did you get those?"

"That farmyard we came through. Didn't you notice the chicken house?" I slipped the eggs into the hot ashes at the edge of the fire.

Thomas chuckled. "I noticed the farmyard, but mostly I noticed the farmer's wife—or daughter, mayhap—standing in the doorway. Bloomin' pretty she was, with a shape—" His calloused hands described opulent curves in the air. "Don't tell me you didn't see her!"

"I was more interested in the chickens in the coop than the chicken in the doorway."

"You're still a youngster, laddie. Wait till you're grown. You'll have more eye for a woman then."

"Could be. I admit the state of my stomach has more importance now." I reached forward with a stick and shifted the eggs slightly in the ashes.

Potter put his arms around his raised knees, and leaned his chin on them. "The first woman a man knows—*knows*—ah! There's nothing else like it!" He gave me a sidelong glance. "But you've never *known* a woman, have you, laddie?"

Deliberately I mistook his meaning. Keeping my face quite straight I answered casually. "You are wrong. There is a girl I know well—very well, in fact. Better, I vow, than you ever knew a woman."

Tom Potter grunted disbelievingly. "Go on with you! You brag! You don't know any more about women than you might learn from a sister."

Suddenly I yearned for a little mischief, a little laughter—no matter how private it had to be. I leaned back on my elbows, my legs stretched out to the fire. "This was no sister, but there was nothing about her I did not know."

Potter glared at me. "At your age? You ought to be ashamed! A boy like you—I don't believe you! Who was she? What was her name? Was she older than you?"

"She was the same age as I. A stubborn wench."

"Spirited, eh? Oh, they're fine when they have some

spirit! What was her name, Robbie? Who was she?"

I sat up and pulled the eggs away from the ashes with the stick. "These are done, I think. Look out for your fingers. They are hot."

"Tell me her name, Rob, or I'll vow you made her up!"

"Her name? Her name was Deborah Sampson. But I have not seen her since I joined the army. Ready for your eggs?"

"I'd much rather a woman like your Deborah Sampson, but since there's no chance of that, I'll take the eggs." He shook his head and chuckled. "You young scoundrel!" he said. "I had thought you such a *pure* boy!"

I could not help it—I laughed aloud. Later I was amused to find that Tom must have spread the word that I was not the quiet infant they had thought me. I seemed to gain some stature in the men's eyes.

20 ☆ The Fever

Strangely enough, my next foray was against our own men. Soldiers who were being retired from the army were discovering that Congress had no money to give them their promised pay, nor did it have power to levy taxes to raise such monies. Angrily they threatened revolt, and General Washington's calm promise to intercede for them only quieted the unrest temporarily. Even he, great man that he was, could not distribute money that did not exist.

In June more trouble erupted when eighty Pennsylvania men, about to be disbanded from the army, stormed into Philadelphia demanding their due. They were joined by two hundred or so equally excited soldiers, and after seizing weapons from the Philadelphia Barracks and fortifying themselves well at the local taverns, they marched on the State House from which a helpless Congress discreetly fled to Princeton in New Jersey.

With Philadelphia in an uproar, General Robert Howe was dispatched on the double with fifteen hundred troops to take control of this situation. Life at West Point having been exceedingly quiet for the past several months, I was one of five men who asked for, and was given, permission to join Howe's men in the city. Off we went, only to find when we arrived that the work had been done. There was naught else for us to do save witness the public flogging of four of the mutineers, and this I chose to avoid.

However, there we were in a city I had never seen, and we agreed to stay a day or so. How much better for me if we had not!

My friend of the "roasted-egg conversation," Thomas Potter (Doubting Thomas who underestimated my knowledge of females!), was one of our small group, and the first day we spent pleasantly in the city. In spite of the military unrest it was a pretty place, with much to see and—gloriously!—much to eat. In one of the inns we heard of some sort of malignant fever that was taking hold among the troops stationed there, and which, we were told, was spreading to the civilian residents, but we paid little heed. Why does one always assume one is immune to all disaster?

I awoke the next morning in a fit of shivering, at the same time sweating as though a bucket of water had been thrown over me. Thomas eyed me with alarm.

"Seems you've been took with that fever," he said.

"Nonsense," I told him. "I shall be all right as soon as I have had something to eat."

I climbed out of bed, took one step toward my boots, and fell flat on my face.

"Off to the hospital with you," announced Tom, and slung me over his broad shoulder. Down the stairs of the inn, past the host who backed away from us when Tom said "Fever," and out the door.

"Thomas, put me down! There's naught wrong with me!"

"Put you down? You can't even stand!"

"I can't go to the hospital! Tom, take me back to the inn. I'll be right as a trivet in an hour or so!"

He didn't bother to answer, simply marched along the street, my head hanging miserably over his shoulder, the sweat pouring across my face.

At the hospital, crowded beyond belief with similar cases, Tom was directed to lay me in a loathsome bunk. He looked at it in disgust.

"There is nothing better than that?"

"Be grateful for that one. We just took the last patient out to bury him."

Tom put me down and stood scratching his head. "I'll try to find something better, Robbie," he said, but I barely heard him as I slipped into unconsciousness.

I don't know how long I stayed in that unknowing state before I was roused by voices in argument.

"There is still warmth in his coat," one voice said, "and I lay claim to it."

"You had the last coat. This one is mine."

"But his breeches won't do me no good—he's a lean one, he is. Those breeks would be too tight for me."

"Let's get him out of here. We'll throw dice for his clothes."

I knew who they were—undertakers who were about to bury me. Was I dead? It was possible, although no one who was dead should feel as aching and miserable as I. I tried to speak and could not. It was like a terrifying nightmare. I felt the hands of one grasp my shoulders, while the second took my ankles, and as I was lifted from the bed I managed some sort of anguished sound. The two vultures heard it—I swear they did—but they took no notice until a nurse walked by and I moaned again. The man stopped.

"Where are you taking that patient?" he demanded.

"Potter's Field," replied the voice at my ankles.

"He is alive, you dogs. Put him down!"

"He won't be alive long—look at him! We'll take him off now and give you another bunk for the next one."

"You move that boy and I'll carve your hearts out with my own hands! At least let him die! Now, get out of here!" I was allowed to fall back onto the bunk and had almost slipped into oblivion when I heard the nurse add quietly, "But you may as well come back in an hour or so. He will be ready for you by then."

I seemed to float in and out of thick, suffocating clouds. I could not open my eyes, nor move a muscle, and yet I was aware at some point that a man was speaking to me. His voice was deep and authoritative, and I judged him to be a physician.

"Can you hear me, boy? Can you open your eyes?" I could hear him, but my eyes seemed sealed shut. I felt his hand on my cold, damp forehead—I must feel like a corpse, I thought—and after a few more attempts to rouse me, he turned away. Perhaps he assumed me to be dead, for though I could hear him speaking to other patients in the ward, he wasted no further time on me. If the undertakers were to come back now no one would stop them from taking me away. The dice would be thrown to determine who won my clothes, and I would be thrown into that final resting place for the unwanted and unclaimed, Potter's Field. Inside me the horror grew, made unbearable by my inability to communicate. I struggled in torment and must at last have given voice to some sound, for the doctor was by my bed in an instant.

"I would have sworn . . ." he murmured, and then I felt his hand thrust inside my coat and pressed firmly on the binder that covered my breasts. "Good God!" was all he said.

Lest there be any doubt he slipped his hand gently under the constricting garments and snatched it away as if he had been burned.

"Where's the supervisor?" I heard him ask. "Where's Mrs. Parker, the hospital supervisor?"

And as I slipped again away from reality and into that dark, frightening place of sickness, I knew beyond doubt that Deborah Sampson had been discovered. What would happen to Robert Shurtlieff I had no idea, nor, at that moment, could I care.

Dr. Binney enlisted the aid and a promise of secrecy from an astonished Mrs. Parker, and I was moved to her private quarters and nursed as though I was General Washington himself. Or, perhaps more rightly, *Mrs.* Washington! Dr. Binney often called upon me. I had no choice but to tell him my story, and though I asked no consideration from him, he said he would not divulge my identity.

21 ☆ Betsy

It was more than a week before I could even sit up in bed, idly watching the comings and goings in the hospital through the open door of the room in which I lay. Many kindhearted Philadelphia matrons visited the soldiers who were patients there, sometimes bringing fruit, a cake, or some other sweetmeat. Occasionally one of them would put her head in my door and ask in a sympathetic, muted whisper how I did, and if there was anything she could do for me. I always replied that I was gaining strength rapidly and was well taken care of, at which point she would generally make a "tsk, tsk" sound, murmur, "Poor boy!" and depart.

One afternoon a much younger female darted past my door, looking in as she went by. A second later she reappeared. I judged her to be about seventeen years old, with thick curling brown hair, sparkling blue eyes, and a trim figure.

"May I come in?" she asked.

"Certainly. Sit down." I gestured to a chair.

She sat gracefully, her skirts falling crisply about her. There was a moment of silence. Then——

"You must have been very ill indeed!"

"Why do you say that? Do I look so haggard?"

"Oh, no! Not haggard. Just weak, and rather pale. But you have a room of your own. I thought soldiers were always in large wards."

"How did you know I was a soldier?"

With a pleased smile she indicated my uniform, washed and ironed, hanging on a hook against the wall. "It *was* rather clever of me, wasn't it?" she said.

"Very." I was relieved that we had skirted the reason for my having a private room. "My name is Robert Shurtlieff," I volunteered.

"I am Betsy Langway. I live in Baltimore, but I am visiting relatives in Philadelphia. They told me that hospital-visiting was quite permissible—even patriotic! —and since I have been really very bored—oh, I should not have said that, should I? One should never admit boredom. It betokens a very small mind." She sounded so amusingly pedantic that I laughed aloud. She frowned. "Why are you laughing? It is quite true, you know."

"Perhaps. If it is, my mind must be very small indeed. I have been lying here for days, most definitely bored."

"That is quite different! Being bored is probably good for you, since it indicates that you are getting well enough to want diversion." She pulled the chair an inch closer to the bed. "Shall I sing for you?" she asked seriously. "I sing passably well."

Again I laughed. "I am sure you do, and perhaps some other time——"

"Do you wish me to leave? Have I tired you?"

"Not at all."

"I don't want to tire you. It is just that—well, I am not sure how to behave. I never made hospital visits before, you see."

"You do them very well," I assured her.

"Do I? How kind of you to say so. I do like to talk to people, but men rather frighten me. I wonder why it is I do not find you frightening at all."

I could so easily have told her, and bit my lip to hold it back. After a moment she rose.

"I had best leave you now, but I should like to come back, if I may. You would not mind?"

"Not at all," I said honestly. "You have brightened the day."

She smiled happily. "Thank you. I shall return tomorrow." And out the door she whisked.

I lay smiling, thinking what a pleasant companion she would be with whom to chatter of the latest styles in women's fripperies, or some other female interest, but I had no intention of becoming Deborah Sampson again for a while. I had hopes of rejoining my company as soon as I might be released from the hospital, and there was no time yet to indulge myself with feminine relationships. With a small sigh I settled down to sleep, thinking that masculinity posed more problems than I had supposed.

Betsy reappeared the following afternoon, carrying a basket of the most beautiful fruit I had seen since leaving the Thomases' farm. Huge strawberries nestled against deep green leaves, cheek to rosy cheek with velvety peaches.

"These are beautiful! Wherever were they grown?"

"The relatives with whom I am staying have a garden. The peaches are espaliered against the walls. They catch all the sun and ripen early."

"And these relatives do not object to your spreading their bounty amongst all the ailing soldiers in town?"

"Of course not. And I am not spreading it. These are just for you." She settled herself with her particular little flurry of skirts. "Now I want you to tell me all about yourself. Everything!"

I gulped. "There is really very little to know," I said. "I come from a little village in Massachusetts, I am a private in the army——"

"*Where* in Massachusetts?" she demanded. "What are your parents like? Have you any brothers or sisters? How long have you been in the army? Have you ever *killed* anyone? In a battle, I mean. *Tell* me!"

Reluctantly I answered some of her questions with the story of Robert Shurtlieff which I had used since my enlistment. A little of it was true, a great deal of it was false, but there was no help for it. Robbie had to have some background, and I had given it to him.

At last I resorted to a female ploy and feigned exhaustion under the barrage of Betsy's questions. Instantly her blue eyes were filled with remorse.

"Oh, it is all my fault! I have tired you! I am so thoughtless—do please forgive me. It is just that I find you so easy to talk to——"

"There is nothing to blame yourself for. It is just this cursed fever."

She rose, skirts rustling. "Go to sleep now," she said

firmly. "I shall see you tomorrow." Then she went quickly from the room.

During the next several days Betsy continued to visit, and I enjoyed every minute spent with her. She was amusing, bright, and voluble, and it had been so long since I had talked with another young woman. But I could not rid myself of a nagging guilt for keeping her unaware of my sex. She was not a child, she was a young woman, and I was dismayed by the thought that she might develop foolish notions about me.

However, when Dr. Binney came in one afternoon I put Betsy out of my mind. After a brief examination he announced himself pleased with my progress.

"All you need now is to live easily, rest a great deal, and eat well until you gain back all your strength," he said. "I suggest that you pursue that course in my home, with my family."

"Oh, but sir——"

"You are well enough to leave the hospital, but not yet strong enough to resume your military life—if, that is, you are determined to resume it."

"I am, doctor. It is a pledge I have made to myself."

He sighed. "It disturbs me, you know."

"I can see that it might, but I do beg you not to give me away. Not yet, at least. Please, Dr. Binney!"

"Very well, providing you allow me to keep my professional eye on you for a few weeks longer."

"It is very kind of you. If you are sure I shall be no trouble to your family . . ."

"My wife will be delighted. She likes nothing more

than watching young people devour the food she very capably prepares. She will cluck over you and thoroughly enjoy it. It is settled then. Be ready to leave with me this evening."

And so I was virtually spirited away by Dr. Binney, and what poor Betsy would think if she came calling on me again, I did not know. But there was no way of sending word that I was leaving—she had never mentioned the names of the relatives with whom she was staying—and I told myself that it was just as well to sever the friendship now before it became more difficult to do so.

Life in the Binney home was delightful. In all my years I had never been so cosseted, nor so lavishly fed. Mrs. Binney took pride and pleasure in spreading her table with every known dish, all beautifully prepared and delicious to the taste. I could feel myself getting stronger each day, and the mirror told me I was not as gaunt as I had been in the hospital.

The Binneys' two little girls, Sarah and Adelaide, were bright and well-mannered, and enjoyed me as they would an elder brother, for although the doctor had "explained me" to his wife, they had said nothing to their young daughters. We played mumblety-peg with my jackknife in the thick grass by the house, I pushed them in their swing that hung from a sturdy branch of an oak tree, they showed me where laden raspberry bushes grew near the side door, and we stuffed ourselves with the fruit.

Mrs. Binney joined us for strolls around the city, we attended various public exhibitions, and on one warm, sunny afternoon we joined friends of the Binneys to sail for an hour or so on the Delaware. At the end of two weeks I was as sleek and healthy as a kitchen cat, and nigh to bursting with the need for physical exercise and mental occupation. I searched out the proper headquarters in Philadelphia, reported to them that I was again fit to resume my military duty, and was assigned to join a contingent from the Eleventh Massachusetts Regiment on a land surveyance expedition toward the Ohio River. I returned to the Binneys' house and told the doctor of my plans.

"Are you sure you know what you are doing?" he asked seriously. "It would take only a word to release you from service, you know."

"I know. And I thank you with all my heart for not speaking that word. This is something I must do, Dr. Binney, a voluntary task which I must complete. I chose to enlist as a soldier in the Continental Army, and I choose to serve as a soldier until such time as I am mustered out."

He gazed at me deeply from under his beetling brows, and a trace of a smile touched the corners of his mouth. "Very well," he said at last. "I shall continue to keep silent. It is not as difficult as you might think, since I feel sure no one would believe a word of the story if I told it." He held out his hand to me, and I took it, shaking it warmly. "Whatever else you may be, I think you are a good soldier, Private Shurtlieff. Good fortune to you."

"Thank you, sir," I said.

The next day I left.

22 ☆ The Indian Camp

Led by a Colonel Benjamin Tupper, our group left Philadelphia in Conestoga wagons that rumbled, jounced, and bumped their way along, while we sat together under the curved canvas roof or dangled our legs from the rear. It was a peaceful trip, the other men were pleasant, the weather was good, and I was grateful to be free and on my own again. "I'm Deborah Sampson, I'm strong and I'm free." Well, in any case, stronger.

Colonel Tupper's orders read to stop in Baltimore for supplies, and we were told there would be a delay of some hours, during which we might enjoy the city. It was a relief to stretch our legs, and two other men—a Daniel Hayes and a Zadoc Crane—set out with me. Presently we found ourselves in an attractive shopping area, and we strolled from window to window, gazing at the vast array of goods on display.

"Look there," Dan Hayes said as we came to the establishment of a gentleman's tailor. "That patterned waistcoat! Did you ever see the like? Just wait until I rid myself of this uniform—I shall dress like a popinjay!"

The next shop had a selection of women's wear in its window, and I felt a great desire to stop and feast my eyes on dainty handkerchieves and gloves, a delicate pink scarf, bottles of eau de cologne, and other female enticements, but my companions showed little interest. As we moved away from the shop the door opened, Betsy Langway emerged, took one look at me, said, "Oh!" and dropped her parcel. I stooped to pick it up, but the cursed paper unrolled and a pair of frilled white drawers tumbled to the ground. Betsy snatched them up, thrust them behind her, and said, "Robbie!"

"Hello, Betsy."

"I thought you had died! You were not in the hospital, and no one would tell me where you had gone—and I thought you were dead!"

Great tears sprang to the blue eyes, and her voice broke. Dan Hayes and Zadoc Crane were vastly interested in this conversation, and stood grinning at my side. I introduced them, but Betsy paid little attention beyond the amenities.

"What are you doing here?" she demanded. "Why didn't you let me know where you were? Do come home with me now—I want you to meet my family."

"Really, I cannot. I must be back with the others——"

Dan Hayes, drat him, interrupted gleefully. "You have at least two hours, Rob—you cannot refuse such a charming invitation!"

"Certainly not," Zadoc agreed. "I am sure the time would be better spent with Mistress Langway than in gazing in shop windows. We will see you later on."

And heartlessly, though, I am sure, with the best

intentions, the two left us. Betsy, suddenly aware that she was still holding the offending drawers, blushed furiously.

"Turn around, Robbie," she commanded, "whilst I wrap these again."

Her embarrassed fingers made a botch of the job and at last I took paper and undergarments from her and made a tidy package, which I handed her.

"You don't look at all shocked," she said. "Have you ever seen a woman's—unmentionables before?"

"You forget I have sisters," I said honestly. "Even had I not, I should have assumed that females wore *something* beneath their skirts."

Betsy giggled. "You are scandalous! You must not speak that way in front of my parents."

"Betsy, I really do not think I should speak in front of your parents at all. I think it would be much better if I just said it has been pleasant to see you again, and good-bye."

"Oh, please come and meet my family. They have heard me speak of you so often, and they will be just as glad as I that you are alive and well."

What was I to do? If I could have sat with Betsy, talked with her as women talk, asked how she managed the careful arrangement of ringlets on her neck, copied the pattern of the frivolous underdrawers—but Robert Shurtlieff could not do such things! I had set myself up as a man, and I had learned how to behave with other men, but a man's behavior with a woman was something quite different and I had no desire to attempt it! Had I been braver—or wiser—I would have turned tail and run, but I lacked the courage. Acutely embarrassed and uncomfortable, I walked beside Betsy to the Langways' home.

The Langways' home! Oh, poor Deborah! I was a farm girl, used to simple living. One look at this establishment and I was struck speechless with awe at the impressive facade, the elegant furnishings, and the show of obvious wealth. I became suddenly awkward, and barely avoided stumbling over the thick carpets or bumping into the exquisite furniture. When I was introduced to Betsy's mother my mortification was complete! She was gowned in such furbelows and flounces, panniers and laces as I had never seen. Her neckline was so low it shocked me more than my first glimpse of a naked soldier had done, and the towering structure of hair upon her head reduced me to open-mouthed wonder.

Somehow I managed to cope with a bewildering assortment of cakes and tea, though my hand shook until I was terrified of spilling something on the velvety carpet. I listened to my hostess chatter about how much she had heard of me from Betsy, and how she could well understand it, seeing for herself what a personable young man I was. My only relief came with the discovery that Papa Langway was not at home. I could imagine him leading me into his private study, offering me a glass of port, and asking my intentions toward his daughter. I would have fainted on the floor!

When at last I was able to leave I was made to promise "on my honor as a soldier" to visit again when I returned from the expedition. It was one case when that particular soldier had no honor whatsoever! I took to my heels like a hunted hare and did not stop until I was safely inside one of the covered wagons, with the canvas closed tight and lashed into place. Betsy as a friend for Deborah Sampson would have been a joy, but I had no intention of Robert Shurtlieff ever meeting with her again!

Sometimes riding, sometimes walking beside the wagons for exercise, we made our slow way into Virginia country. We passed beautiful large estates, the houses wide and gracious, the fields well-planted and bountiful. There were long stretches of empty meadows also, where only rough trails wound through for us to follow. It was warm, peaceful, inviting country and I should have regained every ounce of my former strength, but somehow I did not.

After some days we neared the Allegheny Mountains, and enlisted the aid of Indian guides to lead us through this virtually uncharted territory. They were friendly, knowledgeable about the country, and businesslike in taking us on our way. Their English was understandable, if not fluent, but they spoke little, even among themselves. From time to time we came to Indian encampments, where we would change guides, picking up new ones and leaving the others to make their way back to their own firesides.

To my dismay, the fever I had suffered in Philadelphia seemed to be recurring, and each day I felt more wretched than the one before. My head ached abominably; I felt hot and flushed and constantly thirsty. I had no energy to walk, stumbling instead of keeping up the pace. At last someone got word to Colonel Tupper that one of his men was in poor health, and he came back to visit with me. After a few questions he delivered his directive in a manner that left me no choice.

"You will stay at the next Indian camp we come to, laddie, and get yourself well again. The area west of here is little known, and I will take no risk of losing you from insect bites, or rough trails, or over-fatigue. We will stop for you on our way back."

There was little to say, and in truth I was relieved at the thought of lying still rather than jolting along in the Conestoga wagon, or trying to keep up with them on foot.

And so, within the next day or so, when we arrived at another Indian camp, I was left there with instructions from Colonel Tupper that I be tended and allowed to rest until the return of the expedition. Looking at the sober dusky faces around me I felt a touch of uneasiness as I watched the wagon train continue on without me, but every bone in my body ached with such violence that I forgot any misgivings when I was shown to a bed of branches, leaves, grasses, and blankets, which I found to be surprisingly comfortable. For the next week I did little but sleep, which I have found to be nature's wise way of restoring health to ailing bodies.

As I improved I took interest in the foods I was served, all of them palatable but many unidentified, and in the various decoctions I was given to drink. Some of these were made by boiling unfamiliar wild herbs or tree barks or other growing things for long hours and straining them from the liquid, thus leaving a sort of broth. It was frequently bitter, but it must have had a salutary effect on me, for the fever vanished completely and strength began to return. It was not long before I wandered freely about the camp, watching with interest the daily occupations of both men and women, and learning much from them.

I was given instructions in shooting arrows from taut bows and did rather well at it, feeling smug and proud when I brought down a deer during a hunting party with a group of the men. The women taught me their ways of making soft leather foot coverings, called moccasins, and I learned the ingredients of many of the medicinal potions I had been given. With so many hours spent in the warm summer sun my skin grew almost as dark as the Indians', and before the expedition returned for me I was completely restored to my usual vigorous health.

23 ☆ Betsy Again

The trip back to Baltimore with the wagon train seemed easier than the outgoing trip had been, and although the men who had stayed with the expedition had tales to tell of the country west of us, I had much to report of my weeks with the Indians. By the time we arrived back in the city we were all eager for its sights and sounds after so much time spent in the wilderness. Again we had hours to spend in Baltimore before continuing on to Philadelphia, where the expedition would be disbanded. When my wagon pulled to a halt I jumped from the back of it and was face to face with Betsy Langway.

"Oh, Robbie—I am so glad to see you! I have been here every day, asking when you would return."

My mouth fell open and I prayed that the ground would do likewise so that I might sink out of sight. Taken completely by surprise I could muster no arguments against her forceful invitation and I was led off, willy-nilly, like a lamb to the slaughter. Once more I went through the agony of tea and flattery from Mistress Langway, until at last Betsy and I were left alone in the drawing room. She approached me with a package in her hands.

"Open it. It holds something I made for you while you were away."

"Betsy—please—no!"

How powerful is a small woman! "Open it," she ordered, and fearfully I unwrapped the covering. There lay six of the finest linen shirts I had ever seen, beautifully stitched and frilled. *Men's* shirts. I put the package down and backed away, my hands behind me.

"Betsy, I cannot. Not possibly."

"Nonsense! Of course you can. I shall be very hurt if you do not."

I stood and looked at her with dismay, and knew that I had no choice. "Sit down, Betsy," I said. "There is something I have to say to you." With her guileless eyes fixed on mine, she sat, like an obedient child. "Betsy, I am not at all what you think. I am a female —very much a female! For my own reasons—because I loved a young man who was killed by the British—I have served as a soldier for more than a year now. It is something I wanted to do for him. Dr. and Mrs. Binney know my story, as does the supervisor of the hospital, Mrs. Parker. That is why I was being cared for in her private apartments. I can only beg of you to keep the secret."

I stopped, holding my breath, waiting for her reaction. Her eyes were enormous, and moved over me as if they had never seen me before—which, in truth, they had not. When she rose, hands clasped together,

I braced myself for whatever hatred or scorn she might pour on me, knowing I would have no right to blame her.

"I think that is the most romantic story I ever heard!" she breathed. "Oh, you poor, dear creature! What a wonderful man he must have been!"

Absurdly my eyes filled with tears, and all my love and hopes and loneliness came back in a great rush of emotion. In an instant she was beside me, thrusting her handkerchief into my hand.

"There now," she murmured, "it has been hard, hasn't it? Being always brave, and saying nothing, and missing him so dreadfully! I think you are the most wonderful woman I ever knew!"

I wiped my eyes and blew my nose, and tried to smile. "And you don't think less of me for not putting you right when we first met?"

"How could you have?" She moved away from me, her face thoughtful. "You know, it is very odd, but I never really thought of you as a man—only as someone I liked a great deal. I am always terribly shy with men, and I found I could talk so easily to you. And now I see why!" Suddenly she laughed joyously. "Oh, what a lark! To think that a woman could be smart enough to fool all those men! How clever of you!" She whirled on me. "I will never tell—I promise you! And if I see you ever again whilst you are still in uniform I shall flutter my eyelashes at you and make your comrades think you are a positive devil with the ladies!"

It was my turn to laugh. "Don't you dare! I have enough trouble pretending to be a man without that!"

She snatched up the parcel of shirts and held it out to me. "I do want you to have these," she said. "You must be the best-dressed soldier in the Continental Army."

"Oh, Betsy—really—I cannot——"

"Yes, you can! I do like you so much—what is your name?"

"Deborah Sampson."

"I do like you so much, Deborah, and I am so proud of knowing a woman like you! There!" She placed the package in my hands. "They are yours." Then her brows knitted in thought. "Whatever shall I tell my parents? I am sure they believed I was becoming interested in you."

I grinned at her. "Tell them you found I was not all you had thought me," I suggested, and she laughed aloud. Then her face sobered.

"Take care of yourself, dear friend. I shall think of you often." She held out her hand and I took it, and then she leaned forward impulsively and kissed my cheek. "If you ever long to escape from your make-believe man's world and spend an hour or so in woman-talk, come and see me."

"Thank you," I said. "Someday I may."

And with my heart feeling a great deal lighter I left the house, while Betsy stood waving at the door.

24 ☆ Petticoats Again

In September of that year, 1783, the Treaty of Paris was signed, assuring peace to a weary America. My regiment, the Fourth Massachusetts, was to be disbanded and I was ordered to return to West Point for the occasion. I had been spending a few days with the Binneys in Philadelphia, and the whole family came to the coach station to see me off. As we stood waiting for the stage to depart, the doctor handed me a sealed letter.

"Give this to Major General Paterson at West Point," he directed. "I feel that now, when your position in the army is no longer threatened by discovery, I must admit my knowledge of your secret."

"But Dr. Binney, sir—will that not make me of special interest? Could I not simply be mustered out as I was taken in? Is there any need for my officers to know?"

"Yes, I think there is. Please, do as I say."

"Yes, sir. If you insist. And thank you, Dr. Binney—for everything!"

I offered him my hand, which he shook heartily, and then I climbed into the coach and off we clattered.

Looking back through the small window I could see all the Binneys waving after me.

It was gray and foggy, with spattering rain, when we arrived in Elizabeth Town, in New Jersey. In addition to the knapsack hung over my shoulders, in which I had put Dr. Binney's letter, I had a small trunk. Five of Betsy's beautiful shirts were in it—I was wearing the sixth—some smallclothes, a daily journal which I had managed to keep with reasonable regularity, and a few other personal items. With my trunk under my arm, I joined a number of other passengers on a boat bound up the North River.

I could have gone inside the little cabin, but I preferred to place my trunk on deck, sit on it, and think. It was hard to believe that my "adventure" was almost over. Upon arriving at West Point I would be discharged from the army. What I might do then I had not the least idea. I sat in the chill damp afternoon, and for the first time I wondered what good—if any—I had done for Robbie or for my country. Was anyone the better off for my having served as a soldier? Would there have been the slightest difference in the outcome if I had spent the time spinning in other women's kitchens, teaching other women's children? The answer was "No." And yet I knew I could have done nothing else. At that particular time at which I enlisted, under the conditions that were then in effect, with my own heritage of dedication to my country, with the deep love and grief I had felt for Robbie Thomas—there had been no choice for me. Even now, looking back on the hunger and thirst and fatigue, at the wounds, the fever, and my personal loneliness, I would not have undone it if I could. I knew now how Robbie had lived and died, and what he had died for. It made him forever a part of me.

Suddenly I shivered. The wind had become a gale as I sat thinking, and now the rain battered down in force. In an instant I was soaked through and chilled to my marrow. Thinking to find shelter in the cabin I rose and started to lift my trunk when the vessel gave a sickening lurch and the slippery deck slanted sharply toward the water. With nothing to cling to I slid helplessly across the deck, was catapulted over the railing, and landed in the river. A moment later the little craft keeled over in such a manner as to create an enormous wave which pushed me roughly toward the nearby shore. Thank fortune the river was narrow at that place! I have never been a good swimmer, and I might well not have reached land if that giant surge had not propelled me so close to the blessed solidity of the river bank.

The other people on the boat were as lucky as I, and we all reached safety with no worse hardship than quaking fright and a chilling bath. My trunk was lost with the little ship, which settled quickly at the bottom of the river—good-bye to Betsy's linen shirts!—but my knapsack was still strapped to my shoulders. We were all speedily picked up and set aboard a small cruising boat, which prudently clung to the cover of the river banks until the storm was over. It then returned us to Elizabeth Town, where we spent the night at an inn, drying our clothes and warming our bodies, before re-embarking the following day. That second brief voyage was successful, and again I was at the Fortress of West Point.

In due course, and with deep misgivings, I reluctantly presented Dr. Binney's letter to Major General John Paterson, who, upon reading it, looked at me in disbelief, and promptly sent for the regimental commander, Colonel Henry Jackson, who had succeeded Colonel Shepard. They walked to the far side of the room, shaking their heads and muttering together, while I stood at attenion, my heart thudding.

At last Major General Paterson approached me, his hands behind his back, his brow drawn into a frown. He cleared his throat and I stood a trifle straighter.

"Hmmm!" he began. "Colonel Jackson and I find this letter from Dr. Binney difficult to believe."

"Yes, sir," I said.

"And yet we feel that surely Dr. Binney, a *medical* man, would not be—er—mistaken."

"No, sir."

"If it is true, we are both quite—*shocked!*"

"I am sorry, sir."

"Do you not feel that we have reason to be?"

It was a direct question and demanded a reply. I looked at him, my eyes almost level with his own.

"No, sir, if you will pardon me, I do not think so. There has been no moment in my months in the army when I have behaved in any manner other than that befitting a soldier."

Colonel Jackson fired the next round. "Are you telling me, Private Shurtlieff, that—that——" The poor man looked agonized. "That you have also behaved in a—a—a *virtuous* manner?"

"Yes, sir. I am."

"You maintain that you are of the female sex, that you have spent months in totally male surroundings, that your sex has not once been discovered by your fellows nor—exploited by them?"

"Yes, sir. That is precisely what I maintain."

There was a pause while the two men stood and stared at me. Then Major General Paterson pulled out a chair.

"Sit down, Private Shurtlieff."

I sat.

I was then subjected to a barrage of questions, the while they made notes on my answers. Upon coming to West Point who had been my drill sergeant? Sergeant Calvin Munn, Fourth Massachusetts Regiment. Sergeant Munn's name was written down and I knew he would be questioned. (He was, and declared that I "was prompt and expert, and did my duty faithfully as a soldier.") What action had I seen during my enlistment? I told them. What was the nature of the illness that put me into the hospital in Philadelphia and into Dr. Binney's care? I told them that. In short, they questioned my every movement during the time I had served as a soldier, and in every case I answered truthfully.

At last they conferred privately again, and then Colonel Jackson left the room. It must have been half an hour later when he returned, bearing a large basket filled with female clothing. In spite of the dubious situation in which I found myself I could not help but be amused when I considered how he must have obtained the garments. From his wife, I supposed, but what could he have told her? "There is a young soldier who requires a change of clothing, my dear. Will you outfit him, please, with some of yours?" Poor woman! What must she have thought?

I was given a room in which to change, something I felt a strange reluctance to do. However, whether in petticoat or breeches I assumed I was still under military orders, and I did what I could to present a not unlovely feminine picture. It had been a long time since I had felt the soft swing of skirts against my legs, and as I moved about the room I found I was taking the long strides to which I had become accustomed in hours of marching. It required intense effort to shorten my step to one proper for a woman. When I unbound my bosom and fastened myself into the borrowed bodice I was embarrassed by the sudden emergence of my female figure. My breasts were lifted and emphasized by the stiff boning in the dress in a way that made me exceedingly self-conscious.

I unbraided my pale hair from the queue in which I had worn it for so long and combed it into some semblance of female order, partially hiding it under a bonnet. There was little I could do about my calloused, rough hands with their broken nails except try to conceal them in mitts. The shoes that had been provided were small, but they did at least make me constantly aware that I must take shorter steps. At last, having done all I could do, and feeling something of a fool in such unfamiliar finery, I opened the door to the room where the two officers waited for me.

Unwilling as I had been to shed my uniform, I was woman enough to be flattered by the stunned surprise on their faces. I was then escorted around the grounds, Major General Paterson on one side and Colonel Jackson on the other. Oh, Private Shurtlieff, what privileged company you find yourself in!

Officers and enlisted men were everywhere, all the Fourth Massachusetts Regiment gathered together, awaiting the discharges that would come in a few days. We passed Thomas Potter sitting outside his tent, cleaning his musket, and though he looked up as we walked by he showed no recognition. Men with whom I had marched, eaten, hungered, swapped stories, joked, dressed, and slept gave me no more than the normal interested glances they gave any woman. The two officers escorting me looked at each other. "Incredible!" they murmured.

There was, of course, no possible way to keep the story quiet now. I was given a private apartment, which I found very lonely, and clothing for either sex. Whenever possible I chose to wear my regimental uniform. It felt more familiar, it made me less conspicuous in that masculine stronghold, and it seemed more truly my own. All in all, I was living in some sort of limbo. Was I man or was I woman?

That was a question many people wanted proven. In my uniform I met Tom Potter and this time he knew me.

"Robbie!" He stepped back a pace, looking at me. "Pshaw! It's not true, is it, boy?"

"Yes, Tom, I'm afraid it is."

"But it can't be! I'd have known, Robbie—I'd have known! Why, we've slept side by side! I'd have *known,* Robbie!"

"But you didn't, Tom. I wish you didn't know now. It makes everything quite different, doesn't it?"

He gazed at me, and then his weathered face cracked in a broad grin. "You recollect telling me one night about that girl you knew? The time you filched the eggs right out from under the hen while I was sizing up the farmer's wife? Remember that time, Rob?"

"I remember. You didn't believe me then, either."

"That girl you talked about. You was just talkin' about yourself, wasn't you?"

"Yes. I had to put you in your place, Tom. You were getting too cocky about all your conquests."

"And all the time there was one right beside me and I never knew!" He shook his head. "Seems like I don't believe it even now! What shall I call you now, Robbie? What was that name you told me? That girl's name?"

"Her name was—is—Deborah. But I'd rather be Robbie, Tom—as much longer as I can."

And that was the way it went. I am sure that to this day many of those men who knew me as Robbie, and later found me to be Deborah, will never believe that I came through those military months with my "honor unblemished and my virtue unstained."

25 ☆ Ben

On October 23, 1783, along with many others, I was given an honorable discharge from the Continental Army by General Henry Knox. Wasting no time, I boarded a sloop headed for New York City, with no very clear idea of what I would do when I reached there. I simply wanted to get away, to discover for myself who I was, and decide what was to happen next.

In New York I learned of a packet boat headed for Providence, Rhode Island, and from there I started on foot northeast toward Boston. I still wore my uniform, partly for comfort and practicality, and partly because it made it easier to travel alone. I was totally free, and perversely I regretted the fact. I found myself wishing for some tie, some relative, someone who would acknowledge me as more than a homeless, rootless being. After my disgrace at Sproat's Tavern, it would have been impossible for me to face Mrs. Thomas again. It may have been this need for a family that took me to the home of an aunt, Alice Waters, in a Massachusetts town called Sharon.

It takes a great deal to startle New England farm

folk, but both my aunt and uncle took my story so unquestioningly that I was surprised.

"We have heard some talk of it, Deborah," Aunt Alice said, and her husband grinned.

"Yes. Seems that Baptist church you joined didn't hold with such goings-on," he announced. "Seems you were excommunicated."

I gasped. "Excommunicated? From the church? Dear heaven! Why? And how did you hear of it?"

"That kind of news travels, Deborah," Aunt Alice said. "I don't know that we got the straight of it, of course."

"Most likely you did," I groaned. "What did you hear?"

"Heard tell you were accused of dressing in men's clothes and enlisting as a soldier in the army . . . heard you behaved very loose and un-Christian-like . . ."

"Oh, Lord!" I remembered my disgraceful return from Sproat's Tavern, supported by Ezra Henderson and another of my Baptist "friends."

Uncle Waters leaned over and patted my hand. "Don't take it so to heart, child. I'm not sure any church has the right to pass such judgments—to tell a body what he should or shouldn't do—not if that body isn't hurting anyone. Seems to me that's one of the things we built this country for—a personal freedom in churchly matters."

"That is a comforting thought," I said weakly. "I thank you for it. Was there more? I had better know it all."

"Oh, something about some of the brethren had labored with you to repent of your ways——"

"Oh, they did! They wanted me to kneel and pray. I could not!"

"And that you had left those parts in a secret manner and no one knew where you had gone——"

"I thank my stars for that, at least! And so I am excommunicated?"

"Unless you wish to return and make—ah—'Christian satisfaction.' "

"Thank you, no. In any case, they would never understand it. I am not sure I understand it myself." I looked at those two kind faces. "Would you rather I did not lodge here with you?"

Aunt Alice's voice was indignant. "What rubbish you talk, Deborah! Of course you will stay here! Your uncle and I will welcome some young blood around the house."

And that is all that was said of my religious downfall. What distress it must have caused Mrs. Thomas! I still grieve over that.

I was accepted into the Waterses' house, and given my own chamber, and before more than a few weeks had passed I was asked to teach in a Sharon school. I made one or two simple dresses, and in these I spent the days in the classroom. Often I put on my old breeches and worked on the Waterses' farm, but Robert Shurtlieff had been left at West Point, and I was unequivocally Deborah Sampson.

A lonely Deborah Sampson, to boot. As I stood in

front of my little classroom each morning and looked down at the fresh young faces I wondered whether the rest of my life would be spent teaching other women's children. Would I never have any of my own? I yearned to know a woman's pride in bearing a child, in mothering a child, in *loving* a child. Each evening when I returned to the quiet house that my aunt and uncle so generously let me share, I longed for a home of my own—where I would be mistress, not guest. My own pots and kettles, my own bed and board, my own bits and pieces. No, not *my* own, *our* own. It could never be Robbie, but there had to be someone somewhere to share such treasures with, someone to love and work with, someone who would love *me!* I was a lonely Deborah Sampson, indeed, and one who was ripe for understanding and affection. For love.

The long lonely winter passed, and spring had come with its promise of new life. My aunt and uncle had driven into the village one afternoon and I was in the kitchen preparing the "maids of honor" tarts that Aunt Alice so enjoyed. I stood by the table, mixing the rich filling of eggs and sugar, flour and butter, ground almonds and sherry wine, when I heard the sound of a horse's hoofbeats on the dirt road. Thinking to see my relatives home again I looked through the open door. A sleek horse came trotting into the dooryard, and as the rider swung one long leg over the saddle and stepped down, I gasped. It was as though time had suddenly peeled away, leaving a younger Deborah sitting on a stone wall in winter sunshine, holding that first letter from Robbie and mopping her tears with a borrowed handkerchief. Here came that tall, dark-haired man, owner of the handkerchief, wearing the same disreputable hat. The laugh wrinkles were deep around his eyes and his mouth curved in a smile as he approached the open door calling cheerily, "Waters?"

I came close to knocking the pastry-lined patty pans to the floor!

He stepped inside, his jaw dropped, and we stood gaping at each other.

"Mistress Sampson!" he said.

"Aye."

For a moment he stood silent, hat in hand, gazing at me. Then, with his steady eyes still on mine, he said, "I grieved to hear of Corporal Thomas."

"Thank you." There was no quaver in my voice now. All the tears I would ever shed for Robbie had come and gone, long ago. The golden memory, yes. But no more tears. "How come you here?" I asked.

"I am a friend of the Waterses. They *do* still live here?"

"Of course. Alice Waters is my aunt. They have very kindly taken me in since I returned from—" I paused. Did he know where I had been? What I had been doing?

"From the army," he finished. "Yes, I have heard. I found it hard to believe."

"Hard? Why?"

"The Deborah Sampson I saw seemed—all woman. I could not conceive of her as aught else. Although—" That deep grin lighted his face. "She must have cut a delightful figure in breeches. I would have given much to see that."

"I don't recall my fellow soldiers finding it remarkable," I said flippantly, spooning currant preserves into the patty pans.

He laughted. "*I* would have known," he said. "I swear to you that *I* would have *known!*"

"And I vow that you would not! I was an admirable soldier!"

"That I do not doubt. Whatever you do, Mistress Sampson, you would do admirably. But tell me—did you never weaken? Was there never a time . . ."

Suddenly I bethought myself of that dreadful dark night in the regimental outhouse—the first night I had spent at the Fortress—of my doubts and tears, of my recollection of his words to me when last I had seen him, and of the hysterical laughter that had overtaken and helped me. Just remembering it brought the laughter to my throat again, and bite my lips as I would, I could not hold it back.

"Yes, there was a time," I began, and then another wave of giggles erupted, impossible to conceal.

"An amusing time, I gather," he said, one dark eyebrow raised quizzically. "May I not share it?"

"I cannot tell you, I simply *cannot!* Believe me—if it were possible—" And then, as is the dreadful way with suppressed laughter, it became too much for me and I tipped my head back and laughed aloud until the tears ran down my cheeks. The memory of Deborah Sampson, sitting forlornly in a deserted outhouse in the middle of the night, dressed in her gentlemanly undergarments and thinking of this very man—it was ludicrous! After a moment the laughter caught him too. He chuckled, and then his full laugh joined mine and we rocked about the kitchen, holding our sides, completely out of control. That was the moment when Aunt Alice and Uncle Waters arrived home.

To say that they were bewildered would be an understatement. They stood looking at us as if we had both gone mad. At last I wiped my eyes, tried to breathe deeply, and fought back the last bits of laughter. The man turned to Uncle Waters.

"Ah, good afternoon, friend Waters. I wonder if you would be good enough to introduce me to your niece."

My uncle stared at him. "You mean you and Deborah are not acquainted?"

"Not formally."

"Well! Deborah, this—ah—this is our friend, Benjamin Gannett. Our niece, Deborah Sampson, Ben."

Mr. Gannett turned to me and bowed slightly, smiles still tugging at his lips. "Mistress Sampson."

I curtsied. "Mister Gannett."

Shaking her head in puzzlement, Aunt Alice sighed. "I do not understand it," she said, "but you had best stay and sup with us, Ben. You seem to find each other excellent company."

"Thank you, Alice. I accept with pleasure. Your niece is—stimulating, to say the least."

Presently the two men left the house to walk the farmstead and talk together, and Aunt Alice and I began the preparations for supper. She kept eyeing me speculatively, and at last she spoke.

"You had not met Ben Gannett before, Deborah?"

"We had met—in a way—but I did not know his name." I described the times he had brought us news of the Thomas boys. "It was such a ridiculous thing that set me to laughing—I could not tell him of it, nor can I tell you. He must think me a complete ninny to be so undone by laughter."

"Not likely. No one enjoys a hearty laugh more than Ben Gannett. He's a high-spirited man—a good man, too. Shiftless, some say, but good withal." She set her good blue and white plates carefully on the table, and then added in an implausibly casual manner, "Never could make out why Ben hasn't married. Plenty of girls would have taken him. He is honest, well-spoken, good-hearted—just a mite shiftless is all."

I touched her cheek lightly, leaving a trace of flour from my fingers, and our eyes met. I smiled. "Thank you, Aunt Alice." She had the grace to blush. "There are worse faults than shiftlessness, I think," I went on. "Far worse. I will put the tarts in the oven. Then if you could spare me for a few moments—my hair——"

We shared the conspiratorial smile of two women with a single thought. "Of course, child," she said. "Take your time. 'Twill be a while yet before the meal is ready."

I closed the door of my chamber and plumped down on the edge of my high bed in a whirl of skirts. "Well, Deborah Sampson!" I thought. "Perhaps you have a second chance! How strange that it should be *that* man—that Benjamin Gannett man! He has crept into your thoughts at such odd moments—and now—well!"

I brushed my pale straight hair until it shone—no more the tight, greased queue of Robert Shurtlieff!—and pinched my cheeks to pink them. I wished I had a newer and prettier frock, but there had seemed little reason. Suddenly now I cared about my appearance again as I had not done in months. I found a fresh white fichu to tuck in my bodice, changed my work shoes for lighter slippers, and brushed a damp fingertip across my brows, wishing they were darker. Then, with a last —and not wholly dissatisfied—look at myself in the mirror, I joined the others for supper.

The small efforts I had made must have been of some use, for as we sat at the table I saw again in Benjamin Gannett's eyes that bolstering, flattering approval I had seen before. It made me feel proud, and a little skittish, but at the same time vulnerable. I *cared* what this man thought of me. When at last he left the house he murmured something about ". . . call again soon, if I may."

Bewildered, Uncle Waters looked at him. "Of course, Ben. Why not?"

"Yes, do, Ben," Aunt Alice said enthusiastically. "Come back soon. And often!"

As for me, I simply smiled at him. My *warmest* smile!

For the next several days I primped, kept myself constantly fresh and unrumpled, and listened for hoofbeats. Aunt Alice looked at me sympathetically, but said nothing. Uncle Waters was totally unaware of anything unusual. At last, when nigh to a week had passed, and I was out of sorts with the unpredictability of mankind in general and Benjamin Gannett in particular, I pulled on my old breeches, tied my hair back with a grubby bit of ribbon, and went to work at loosening the soil around the cabbages. It was a sultry evening, I worked hard with a grim determination not to think of that fickle Gannett fellow, and in half an hour my hair was escaping in damp, straight strands, my shirt was soaked with perspiration, and my hands were filthy. That, of course, was when Ben arrived. There he came ambling down across the field from the house, the battered hat on the back of his head and a long blade of grass between his teeth.

"I was quite right," he announced. "I knew the breeches would be becoming."

Perversely, I was furious with him. Why could he not have presented himself when I was dressed for him? Expecting him? Eager to see him? Oh, no! He must wait until I looked my worst, until I was completely off-guard and unprepared!

"I wear the breeches because they are practical," I said in my chilliest voice, "not because they are becoming."

"But how fortunate that they can be both," he said imperturbably. He removed the disgraceful headgear and fanned himself with it. "Do you never stop working?" he asked. "It is much too warm to work so hard."

I dug the hoe into the ground as hard as I could. "I don't consider this as work. I like to grow things. I always have."

"I like watching things grow—which is quite different." He took the hoe from my hand and dropped it on the ground. "Sit down and talk to me. It makes me weary to watch you laboring away. I have a very lazy temperament, you know. I deplore the necessity of working for a living."

His voice was deep, and seemed always on the verge of laughter, just as his dark eyes crinkled at the corners with constant amusement. It was impossible to maintain my annoyance at his ill-timed arrival, and so, defeated, I sat on the ground beside him, my knees drawn up and my arms around them.

"You prefer that the wherewithal of life just be dropped in your lap?" I asked.

"Precisely. And I demand very little. But even that, it seems, I must scratch for."

"From what my uncle tells me your 'scratching' must be effective. He says you were more than generous in contributing grain and cattle and horses during the war."

"I did not say I lived without working. I simply said I would prefer to."

How comfortable it was just to be with him! His acceptance of my soiled, sweat-damp clothes, his ease in talking, his obvious pleasure in being with me—all this began to dispel my long-felt loneliness. His physical presence, the brush of his shoulder against mine, the sight of his strong hand—dark hairs grew on the backs of his fingers—idly pulling at a tuft of grass, the nearness of his face—so close that I could marvel at the thickness of his dark lashes—these things brought back the old, remembered quickening of my pulse, the wonderful, womanly weakening deep within. Once there had been Robbie, but that chance of happiness was gone. Now—now I thanked my God that a second chance had come. I wanted to laugh, to sing, to weep. Instead we talked. Dear heaven, how we talked! It was as if we must know everything of each other without delay. I learned that he had been in one of the companies that responded to that first alarm at Lexington, and that he had seen far more action than I.

"And never even wounded," he said. "Can you imagine not being able to hit a target as big as I am?"

I grinned at him. "I could have done better," I boasted.

In some manner we reached the subject of our families, and I told him my mother had been Deborah Bradford, a great-granddaughter of Governor Bradford, and that my father was descended from John Alden and his wife, Priscilla Mullins.

"Then we may well be cousins," Benjamin said happily. "My mother, Mary Copeland, also counted the Aldens among her forebears. What a loving, productive couple they must have been!"

I laughed, and then, because I felt so close to this big, easy-talking, lighthearted, affable man, I recited for him the verse my mother had written for me.

"I'm Deborah Sampson, I'm strong and I'm free.
My forefathers handed their strength down to me.
John Alden, Miles Standish, helped settle this land,
And Governor Bradford ruled well that small band.
Abraham Sampson, he followed ere long,

And all of these names make me loyal and strong."

I stopped and looked at him, and his face was totally serious. He laid one broad strong hand over mine.

"That has sustained you more than once, has it not, Deborah?" he asked, and for no reason at all I wanted to cry. I nodded, my eyes filling with silly tears.

"How did you know?" I whispered.

"Because I know you. I can guess how often you have been lonely, how often you have felt unwanted and pushed about. You would have needed something such as those lines to give you a sense of yourself. A pride in being who you are. Am I not right?"

Again I nodded. "Yes. But there are not many who would understand."

He pulled my head down against his shoulder. "I will always understand you, Deborah. Always. If you will let me."

And, quite unashamedly, I wept happily into his damp shirt, and gloried in the comforting touch of his hand as he patted my hair.

On October 14, 1784, we posted intention of marriage, and on the seventh day of April, the following spring, when I was twenty-four and Ben two years older, we were married by the town clerk of Sharon. After those many, many years I was lonely no longer.

Last Thoughts

The years with Ben have been such happy ones! Not always smooth nor easy—Aunt Alice was right when she spoke of Ben as "shiftless," and Ben was completely truthful when he told me he deplored the necessity of working for a living—but filled with warmth and trust and laughter. I think of Robbie sometimes, without pain, remembering that first young awakening of love. The memory will always be precious to me. But Ben has given me all I could ever ask of any man. His love, his joy in living—and our children.

Earl Bradford came first, and how proud Ben was (and is) of his son! Then Mary, whom we have always called Polly, and lastly Patience. Our small farm (which I worked more than Ben did because I favored the work and he did not) fed us all, but our clothes were patched and mended, and our shoes, when we wore them, frequently out at the bottoms. The children seemed not to miss the things money might have bought them; they were healthy and happy and loved. And certainly Ben was rarely troubled. But I could not help but fret over a barn that needed repairs, a roof that leaked, a dozen other similar demands. And it was that lack of money that brought me to the second "shocking" thing I did.

It is strange now, in the dignity of my late years, to think that when I was a mature woman I caused almost as much furor by my behavior as the young Deborah did when she enlisted. I dressed in a brand new, well-fitting suit of regimentals and went on a Speaking Tour! Not only did I speak publicly in a number of cities, I also performed the Manual of Arms. That decision was made for me by our good friend and neighbor, Paul Revere, the same man who had ridden off into the night to warn the landholders that the British were marching toward Lexington and Concord. (He later told me that he had been captured by the British that evening and never warned "more than a sleepy cow or two," yet I believe his name will go down in history! He is a remarkable man!) In any event, Paul and Ben and I sat talking one evening and somehow the matter of money, or the lack of it, arose.

"Let Robert Shurtlieff make money for you," Paul said. "I warrant he could!"

"Whatever do you mean?"

"Dress that trim figure of yours in your uniform, shoulder your musket, and go forth and speak to audiences. They would pay to hear you, or I am sadly mistaken."

I was shocked. "Appear in public dressed as a *man?* Oh, no! I couldn't!"

The two men burst into laughter. "You did it before," Ben said. "Why not now?"

So I did. I was forty-two then. I packed my uniform and musket, with a fetching bonnet for my feminine moments, and jounced through ten cities or so in a series of jolting coaches that brought out all the aches in shoulder and groin. But, as Paul had predicted, the people came to hear me, and they paid.

In my first engagement in Boston the program was due to conclude with the singing of "God Save the Sixteen States," and I prayed fervently that He would also keep a protective eye on Deborah Sampson Gannett. He must have, for the tour began triumphantly. In Providence I sat on the stage until it was time for my performance, and chuckled to hear members of the audience murmuring that I was, most certainly, a lad of not more than eighteen years. In Holden I was the guest of my former captain, George Webb, and in Lisle I stayed at the home of John Paterson, the man who had once been Major General at the head of my brigade, and who had been so skeptical of my virtue.

My shoulder ached as I went through maneuvers with my heavy musket, my thigh ached from long standing during performances, my face ached from smiling charmingly at hundreds of people—but I was able to bring home a sizable amount of much-needed cash, and the publicity attendant on my trip was eventually instrumental in bringing me a monthly pension from the "United States Army." That "United States" that I, perhaps, in some small way, helped to create.

All that is over now, all the public display and the private hardships. I am well past sixty, surrounded by grandchildren, deeply loved by my husband, learning to sit quietly and take my ease—something Ben has always done so well. The children pester me sometimes for tales of my army days, but it is becoming dimmer in my mind. I can almost taste the roasted eggs I shared with Tom Potter, but the sickening memory of Nathan's face, blown away by British fire, is all but gone. I can recall the desperation with which I pried the musket ball from my flesh, but the days in the Philadelphia hospital, scourged by fever, are no more than a blur in my mind. Until Betsy Langway walked in. I will always smile, thinking of Betsy. I hope she found a man she "could talk to."

So much to remember and think about!

And no matter how many more years God gives me, there is one thing I shall never forget. I still say it to myself from time to time.

"I'm Deborah Sampson. I'm strong and I'm free."